"Drop the gun and climb down, mister."

It was bad manners to call a cowboy "mister," but Deputy Irish Kempen was in no mood to stand on etiquette after being shot at by a drunk Texas drover.

"No harm meant. I wasn't shootin' at you. Let me ride on out."

"No deal. Get down or be dragged down."

A shout caused Kempen to turn, and he saw another drover whipping his horse forward. With the taste of iron in his mouth, Irish realized that this one aimed to ride him down to save his compañero, and reached for his gun.

But just then, a familiar horseman appeared out of a dark alley, his spotted gray moving with uncharacteristic speed. Irish was saved from having to use his weapon as ol' Patch Russell cut off the charging cowboy and pulled up.

"I got me a Dupont double-aught buckshot here," rasped Patch thickly, "and a fierce hankering to splatter some Texas blood all over this here Nebraska dirt."

The street froze as still as death.

POWELL'S ARMY
BY TERENCE DUNCAN

#1: UNCHAINED LIGHTNING (1994, $2.50)
Thundering out of the past, a trio of deadly enforcers dispenses its own brand of frontier justice throughout the untamed American West! Two men and one woman, they are the U.S. Army's most lethal secret weapon—they are POWELL'S ARMY!

#2: APACHE RAIDERS (2073, $2.50)
The disappearance of seventeen Apache maidens brings tribal unrest to the violent breaking point. To prevent an explosion of bloodshed, Powell's Army races through a nightmare world south of the border—and into the deadly clutches of a vicious band of Mexican flesh merchants!

#3: MUSTANG WARRIORS (2171, $2.50)
Someone is selling cavalry guns and horses to the Comanche—and that spells trouble for the bluecoats' campaign against Chief Quanah Parker's bloodthirsty Kwahadi warriors. But Powell's Army are no strangers to trouble. When the showdown comes, they'll be ready—and someone is going to die!

#4: ROBBERS ROOST (2285, $2.50)
After hijacking an army payroll wagon and killing the troopers riding guard, Three-Fingered Jack and his gang high-tail it into Virginia City to spend their ill-gotten gains. But Powell's Army plans to apprehend the murderous hardcases before the local vigilantes do—to make sure that Jack and his slimy band stretch hemp the legal way!

Available wherever paperbacks are sold, or order direct from the Publisher. Send cover price plus 50¢ per copy for mailing and handling to Zebra Books, Dept. 2898, 475 Park Avenue South, New York, N.Y. 10016. Residents of New York, New Jersey and Pennsylvania must include sales tax. DO NOT SEND CASH.

REVENGE IN LITTLE TEXAS

JASON MANNING

ZEBRA BOOKS
KENSINGTON PUBLISHING CORP.

ZEBRA BOOKS

are published by

Kensington Publishing Corp.
475 Park Avenue South
New York, NY 10016

Copyright © 1990 by Jason Manning

All rights reserved. No part of this book may be reproduced in any form or by any means without the prior written consent of the Publisher, excepting brief quotes used in reviews.

First printing: February, 1990

Printed in the United States of America

TO

K. St. J.

who kept telling me to write the American West; to tell of guns and glory, honor and revenge, the law and the lawless.

Chapter One

Carson Kane checked the sturdy sorrel at the crest of a grass-scattered rise and looked down at the Triangle herd.

For the best part of three months they had pushed twenty-two hundred head of ornery cattle up the trail from Texas. Their destination: the shipping point of Two Rivers, Nebraska. The railhead of the Chicago and North Western. Carson could hardly believe that it was almost over, that trail's end was but a few miles to the northeast. He didn't really want it to be over. That was a little odd, he mused, because up until a few days ago he had been wondering if the ordeal would ever end.

This had been his first push. He was three weeks shy of his nineteenth birthday. For years he had been doing a man-sized job on the ranch, ever since he had been tall enough that he had to stoop to walk under a cow pony's belly. But none of it had prepared him for the assay of manhood that was a cattle drive. Somewhere along the trail he had shucked the last vestiges of adolescence, as though the bones of Carson Kane—the sometimes-swaggering, often prideful, painfully self-conscious boy who was prone to blushing—had been left by the wayside, bleaching in the sun. Yes, somewhere along the backtrail he had ceased to wonder if he was a man. A heavy burden had been lifted from his rangy shoulders.

Sitting on his horse up on that rise he could see the whole long dun snake of the herd, from point to drag, as it curled through the sparse hills. In its wake hung a heavy cloud of dust, the color of cornmeal, suspended in the still, November-brisk air. He was awed by the immensity of their accomplishment. Twenty-two hundred head, every one with a stubborn will of its own, as befitting a Texas dogie. Like every true cowpuncher, Carson had developed a high respect for the longhorn. It was the smartest and the meanest creature on God's good earth, and it was powerfully disinclined to tolerate a herd, for longhorn did not naturally congregate except when confronted by calamity or danger. Herding made the longhorn a nervous beast.

Hence, the ritual of trail-breaking. They had left the Triangle range the last week in August. The first few days saw them driving cow, cowboy, and cow pony to the outer limit of exhaustion, twenty-five to thirty miles at a lick. The risk of stampede was always greatest those first few crucial days, for the cows were disposed to turn around and head home. After a week of eighteen, twenty-hour days in the saddle—often including four hours of night guard—Carson, too, had entertained the notion of shucking it all and going back. When he reached that low-tide point of physical and mental exhaustion he even thought about trying to break an arm or a leg in a fall from his horse. Desperate times required desperate measures, and he would have surrendered everything he owned, or was in line to inherit, for just one night in his own bed.

The fifth night out his father had caught him asleep in the saddle while on herd guard. Tyler Kane reached down, grabbed hold of his son's offside stirrup, and pulled up sharply. Carson woke up greeting the ground with an impact that made him sick.

"You whined like a sick pup two years ago, when I took your brother on the last push and left you behind," Tyler had rasped, his bull voice all iron and scorn. "It appears I was right then to leave you, and wrong now for bringing you along."

That had been a turning point for Carson Kane.

After the first week the pace slowed. On the average they racked up eight to ten miles per day. Nearly a hundred days of bone-jarring, back-breaking labor. Tyler had assigned his boy to one of the drag positions—in any cowboy's opinion, the worst job of a push. At first Carson had been resentful. But he kept his mouth shut and never complained. Choking on the dust of the herd, fighting swarms of horn flies, he pulled his weight day in and day out, hazing the cows that lagged off the pace and catching the stragglers that tried to dodge. Gradually Carson developed a fierce pride in his work, in doing a difficult job well. The resentment faded. Best of all, the attitude of the hired hands toward him changed. Precisely because he *was* the boss's son, almost all the Triangle cowboys just naturally kept their distance. But as the drive progressed and the men saw a boy subtly transformed into a hard-working *hombre* who did his part, the walls of reservation crumbled. Cowboys were the most incorrigible of practical jokers. The night they put a fresh prairie flapjack in his bedroll was a fine moment in Carson's young life. It was a prank that implied acceptance. Carson raised cain and cursed a blue streak fit to raise a blood blister on a rawhide boot, but through it all he was as happy as a lark.

What every man on a drive feared most was stampede. Many things could bring it about: the herd carelessly bedded down too close together, the scent of lobo wolves, natural phenomena such as foxfire and chain lightning. Jayhawkers out to rustle a few head had been known to burn buffalo hair upwind. On a dozen nights the signs of impending stampede had been there. The "scours," they were called: the leaders of the herd snorting and restless, roaming through the herd, inciting riot, until the whole lot were on their feet, all facing in one direction. And the night guards would circle in opposite directions, edgy as they "sang" the Texas lullaby, while the balance of the crew, quiet and subdued in camp, warily monitored the passage of the night, the pony with the surest feet in their string saddled and bridled but a short jump away.

Not once, though, did the Triangle herd stampede.

Still, there were other problems. There always were. Several calves were born on the trail and had to be put to death, and the she-stuff often made trouble after that. Hidehunters rimwalked the herd for several days and nights near the upper reach of the Brazos, only to move on to easier pickings. Little spreads along the way, feeding off the passing herds as was their custom, cost them forty head. The Cherokee, through whose nations they were obliged to pass, levied a tribute, called *wohaw*, of ten cents a head. Tyler Kane chewed them down to six cents, then paid up gladly. Each cow cost him, on the average, a dollar to get to market. But the price per head had gotten better every year for quite a spell, and he had all the reason in the world to anticipate a handsome sell, perhaps as much as sixteen dollars per. They had lost seventy-five crossing the Arkansas, the river running high and hard, but all told they would be, Carson estimated, only about a hundred and fifty cows shy once the stockyard tally was made.

A big "drag," a big success, and Carson Kane was proud down to the roots to be part and parcel of it.

It was easy to see that the other drovers knew their ordeal was nearly over. They could smell the wide-open town of Two Rivers just as surely as a steer could smell distant water after a dry haul. Carson had never been to a trail town, but he had heard the cowboys talk. Anticipation leaped like wild flame in their lusty blood. Two Rivers meant washing away the memories of dust, aching bodies, scant sleep, and gnawing hunger. Vivid memories, burned into their souls with a red-hot brand. Liquor, women, games of chance were there for the taking—and anything else that might tickle a Texas drover's fancy. Two Rivers offered it all in an abundance. The Triangle boys had endured snakes, loafer wolves, and each other for a quarter of a year away from the place they called home, and they had a lot of steam to let out.

Now the "Texas Side" of Two Rivers was going to pay for all that grief and hardship.

Carson wished he could share those high spirits, but thoughts of his older brother nagged at him. Murdoch Kane had accompanied his father on that drive two years ago. He had not come home. Instead, he lay in a dusty grave in Two Rivers' boot hill, shot to death over a card game. A gambler had done the deed.

When given the news, and with tears of grief hot on his cheeks, Carson had demanded to know why his father had not strung the cardsharp up.

"Because your damfool brother drew first," had been Tyler's stony response.

That had been the full extent of his father's description of the tragedy. From Grady Harmon and a couple of the other hands who had been present, Carson gradually learned the details. Murdock had been drinking hard. He had accused the gambler of cheating. Surging to his feet, rotgut-clumsy, Murdock had drawn his gun, only to catch the barrel against the edge of the deal table, and the gambler, brandishing an over-and-under derringer, had put a bullet right between Murdoch's eyes.

"There's trail town politics involved," Carson had been advised by Yuby Wellman, the savvy Triangle foreman and drive *segundo*. The soft-spoken, rawhide-tough, and fair-minded top hand had, in some ways, been like another brother to Carson, notwithstanding the fact that Yuby was black, an ex-Ninth Cavalry "buffalo soldier." "The big men in those towns make their living off the cowboy. They don't want the town to get a reputation and lose the business when the trail bosses turn their herds elsewhere. On the other hand, the saloonkeepers don't want it said that they can't protect their people, and that means the gamblers and the soiled doves. Every cardsharp who expects to ply his trade in a place like Two Rivers works by percentage, with the saloon owner as a silent partner. So anything goes, just about. 'Less you shoot a feller in the back, or gun down an unarmed man."

Eventually the salve of time eased Carson's emotional pain. He had assumed that it had done likewise for his father. Hard to say for certain, as Tyler Kane was not one to bare his innermost feelings to anyone.

Then, a month before the push, Tyler had received a telegram. Carson knew it came from Two Rivers, but he was not told the identity of its sender or made privy to its contents.

Ten days later a man had arrived at the Triangle ranch. He and Tyler had talked privately for over an hour, after which Tyler had introduced him to the hands as Reese. It had been patently obvious to everyone that Reese was no drover. For one thing, he wore a pair of Smith & Wessons. A shootist's guns, more balanced and precise than the average thumb-buster. Tyler had offered nothing more than that Reese would be going along on the push. For three months the gunslinger had ridden and camped apart from the others. He had not done a single lick of work. Nobody liked him, and he cared less.

"What's he with us for, anyhow?" Carson had asked Yuby one night when together they had guarded the herd.

"You haven't got it figured out yet?" returned the *segundo*, with a humorless smile.

"Figured what out?"

Yuby had shrugged, like it really didn't concern him. "Well, I sure ain't no gypsy soothsayer, but I have been known to put two and two together on occasion. I reckon Mr. Reese is along to see that the score is settled and that your brother's death is paid for in kind."

Which was why Carson, sitting his sorrel on the crest above the herd, was feeling skittish about the imminence of trail's end, and why he could not find it in himself to share the giddy exuberance of the other drovers. The push was nearly over, but he suspected that the trouble was just beginning.

Chapter Two

"Tyler, ain't that your boy up yonder on the rim?"

Tyler Kane, astride a leggy bay gelding that he kept at a walk alongside the bucketing chuckwagon, looked over at Banjo Stubbins. Following the direction of the grizzled cook's squinty gaze, he saw the rider far off on the crest of the rise.

"You've got good eyes for a half-loco has-been," Tyler remarked without malice.

Banjo snorted over the unlit corncob pipe that spent most of its time clenched between the world's yellowest teeth.

"Good eyes, my foot! I can still count the eagle hairs in a copperbelly's headdress at a long mile. And you know it, *Mister* Kane." He gave the offside wheeler a good hard whack with the harness leather threaded through his callused fingers. "Ma Stubbins raised herself up an addled fool, I reckon. Only way I can figure out why I've put up working for you all these years. You ain't never in all the time I've had the misfortune of knowing you treated me with the respect that even a speckled pup naturally deserves."

"Smooth out your hackles, Banjo. You have to earn respect."

"Earn re . . .!" Banjo sputtered, feigning outrage. "You're one arrogant sonuvabitch."

One side of Tyler Kane's hard-set mouth twitched. It was as

close as he ever got to a smile.

"Be thankful. You're the only person who gets to talk to me that way and keep breathing."

"Why thank you so very doggone much, *Mister* Kane. You got the milk of human kindness in your veins. Why, I'd put you right up there with the saints like Bloody Bill Anderson and the Hanging Judge himself."

Kane kept his gaze on that distant horseman, pretending to ignore the feisty cook. It was a game, of sorts, that they played. Banjo had been with him from the start of it all, going on thirty years now, and though it wasn't in Kane to come right out and say it, he cared about Stubbins. That put old Banjo in an elite group. There had been Edna, of course. Kane had loved his wife. He had failed to realize the true depth of his feelings for her until God took her away that year cholera had struck Texas so hard. It haunted him, that damned inability of his to wear his emotions on his sleeve, because it had prevented him from adequately demonstrating to her how much she had meant to him. All the words left unspoken made the loss that much more heartbreaking.

And then there had been Murdock. Bitterness deepened the lines at the corners of Kane's gimlet ice-blue eyes. One thing was certain, he had not learned his lesson. He had ridden Murdock hard, for it had been his intent to forge his eldest son into a man strong enough to hold onto the empire that he, Kane, had hammered out of the harsh West Texas plains. All along he had refused to recognize what others clearly saw as a mean, crazy streak in Murdock. He *still* refused to do so. But he had to admit to himself that, as with Edna, he had fallen far short of expressing to his older boy the pride and affection of a loving father. Now it was too late.

Dragging a long breath into his lungs, Kane flexed his shoulders and straightened his spine, refusing to acknowledge the discomfort that a long day in the saddle now brought him. The wiry beard that covered his square-jawed face, once as dark as a *señorita's* glance, was these days salt-and-pepper. He knew the peculiar anxiety of one faced with the incontrovertible fact of life: that Time dallies for no man. He had accomplished much, and of that he was duly proud, but there were a few things left undone. He kept looking up at Carson. A man to make. His gaze swung to the horizon ahead and turned as cold as the grave. And a man to kill.

Banjo threw a few sidelong glances at Kane from under his hat, sensing—the way old saddle partners could—the other's change in mood. It was time to drop the banter. Hard to tell exactly what Tyler was thinking, but Banjo figured it had something to do with young Carson.

"I'm right proud of the boy myself," commented the cook, as if to himself. "He pulled his own freight and then some on this trip, that's plain to see."

Yes, thought Kane. *That's true enough. And I'm proud of him too.* But he would only say, stiffly, "I expected nothing less from him."

Banjo grimaced and gnashed on the mangled tip of his pipe a bit more. He thought of Carson, sometimes, as the son he had never been blessed with. And there had been times, especially when Murdock lived, that he had been more of a father to the youngest Kane than Tyler had seemed capable of being.

"You've held a short rein on Carson for as long as I can remember," said Banjo, knowing that he was climbing out on a limb but compelled by his affection for Carson Kane to do so. "Why don't you loosen up on him, Tyler? If you don't he might bolt on you, sooner or later. Lose him and who you gonna leave the Triangle to?"

Tyler turned on him like a cornered mossback.

"We been together more snows than I care to count, Stubbins," Kane growled. "But don't make the mistake of forgetting your place. You still work for me. And if you take the liberty of telling me how to raise my son again, I'll hogleg you off my payroll so fast you'll think the world turned over."

"Dunno how I have put up with working for an ornery polecat like you for so long, anyhow!" shouted Banjo, screwing up his sunwhacked face. He whipped the team so fiercely that the four-hitch spooked and dusted out. Tyler checked the handsome bay and let the chuckwagon rattle by, the big black Dutch oven clanging against the rear axle and cow chips falling out of the "possum belly" sling.

Kane had little time to reflect on the sudden altercation, for he saw a rider approaching from uptrail, a big-boned cowboy on a sturdy claybank: Yuby Wellman, Triangle foreman and drive *segundo*. Yuby slowed his horse and touched the brim of his hat to Banjo as the chuckwagon thundered by in the other direction. But the cook was too burned up for socializing and so failed to even acknowledge Yuby's presence on earth. Puzzled, Wellman pulled rein and twisted in the saddle to look curiously after the wagon. Tyler moved his horse forward.

"Well?" snapped Kane crossly. "You gonna give me the news I sent you after, or not?"

Yuby turned back and looked Kane squarely in the eye, unruffled by the rancher's attitude. Years of tough and often perilous service in the legendary Ninth Cavalry had instilled in him the notion that he had nothing to fear from any man. When it came to true grit he was every man's equal.

"River won't be a problem," he said. "There's one herd staked out just south of town. Saw the dust of another from some high ground. I'd say it's about two hours behind us and a couple three miles to the west."

Kane nodded. He had learned that he could rely on Yuby's information. The man was a top hand, one of the best Kane had seen in a lifetime of ranching.

"We'll move 'em a few more miles, then bed 'em down," he decided. "Come morning Carson will ride with me into Two Rivers, so you'll have to deal with the jaspers from the Department of Animal Husbandry. I must tend to some other business." His gaze shifted left to survey the flank of the strung-out herd. The passage of twenty-two hundred head was marked by a thick, earth-hugging plume of choking dust riled up by thousands of hooves. Horns clacked and clattered like a passel of telegraph keys. Cows bawled for water. Drovers hazed and hollered.

Yuby had more than an inkling about the nature of that "other business." It gave him a funny feeling at the base of his spine. He had been present on that last drive; he had seen Murdock laid under and he had watched something die in Tyler. But it wasn't really none of his never mind. He pushed his hat back on close-cropped hair and mopped the sweat from his brow with the sleeve of his old blue service tunic. It was unseasonably warm for late November.

"The men are in good spirits," observed Kane.

"It's been a push," said Yuby. "But you've got a fair bunch of boys."

Kane gave that almost-smile once more. He knew that the crew was better than average for two reasons: the fear and respect in which they held the Triangle boss and the leadership of Yuby Wellman. Kane looked at the upper sleeves of the cavalry shirt his foreman wore. The sun had not managed to fade entirely the darker fabric where Yuby's sergeant's stripes had been. Wellman drove the men under his command, but his was a fair hand, and if there was a Triangle puncher who objected to taking orders from a black, it was news to Kane. The crew looked up to Yuby as a cowboy at the top of his craft and did what he told them to.

Another rider was galloping up to join them—Kane heard the beat of a horse's hooves behind him. Before he turned he saw a change in Yuby's expression and guessed at the identity of the new arrival sight unseen.

This one was no drover. He wore a long gray duster and buckskin leggins. A rattlesnake band adorned his flat-crowned, wide-brimmed gray hat. A brace of pistols were tied down on his narrow shanks, the guns of a shootist. The man's hair was lank and black and shoulder-length. A cruel arrogance twisted the angular, bristled features. His name was Reese, and he had come to Kane highly recommended as a mankiller. That was all Tyler Kane knew about him or cared to know.

"I'd best get back to the herd," said Yuby, something as cold and as hard as a knife's blade in his tone. He disliked the gunslinger, disapproved of his presence, and didn't mind letting it show. Turning the claybank more sharply than was necessary, he angled toward left point on the herd, the traditional position of the *segundo*.

Reese brought his lanky dun up alongside Kane's horse. He was seated on a rimfire rig with some fancy hand tooling. Kane was pretty certain that it wasn't the hull Reese had left Texas on, but he did not feel pressed to get the particulars of the acquisition.

"Where the hell you been?" he asked gruffly. It was a rhetorical question, of course, a tactic designed to establish authority, to remind Reese that he answered to Kane.

But Reese seized the opportunity to take the query literally and gave a wolfish grin.

"Cute little farmer's daughter a ways back. Showed me the hayloft."

Tyler got a sour taste in his mouth. "Willingly, I hope. All we need is an irate plowpusher on our backsides. And bear in mind that you're riding my stock. I don't care to have the Triangle brand remembered at the scene of every recent atrocity from here to the Pedernales."

"Don't you worry about that sodbusting jayhawker." Reese looked like the cat that had just dined on the canary.

There was a rumble of discontent deep in Kane's throat. "You been getting paid regular?"

"Every week, like we agreed. But I got my sights set on a tidy bonus just a short reach away."

"You'll get it, if you see the job through. But know this. As long as you put my money in your pocket you belong to me."

The word *belong* rankled the gunhawk, as Kane had known it would.

"What if I get it in my head to ride off?"

"You've been doing just that for months now," reminded Kane caustically.

"One time I might not come back."

"You had better be belly up if that happens. It would be a mistake to muddy my water."

Reese pursed his lips and took another measure of Tyler Kane. The rancher was not afraid of him and he had to respect that.

"Your straw boss don't much care for my company."

"None of my boys do."

"Maybe I should push a few cows. Make 'em feel more kindly toward me." He obviously cared less what the Triangle crew thought of him.

"Stay clear of my men," warned Kane bluntly. "Especially Yuby. He was a buffalo soldier."

"Ain't scared of no nigger."

"You wouldn't live long enough to get scared. Besides, I'm not paying you to punch cows."

"Suits me," shrugged Reese laconically. "But I don't know why you wanted me to eat dust all the way from Texas. Why didn't you just tell me to meet you in Two Rivers?"

"I wanted to be sure you'd be there."

"Why, Mr. Kane, you think I'd take your money and then go back on my word?"

"I don't know you well enough to judge." Kane's tone made it manifest that he had no desire to know Reese that well at all.

Reese shook his right leg out of the stirrup and hooked his leg around the saddlehorn. Slouching in the hull, he shook his head, putting on a perplexed face.

"You're just a hard man to please, Mr. Kane."

"You know what to do about that."

"Lee Stanhouse." The shootist smiled at the darkness the name put on Kane's features. "I might've come on up and done the deed by now. He could be cold in the grave and you could rest easy."

"I aim to be there. I want to see him planted right next to my boy."

"How do you know he's still in Two Rivers? Could be he's

moved on. Lot can happen to a man in three month's time. Especially in a trail town. Gamblers just don't stay rooted in any one place too long. It's not healthy."

"He'll be there," grated Kane, as if, since he willed it, it would be so. A deep-flowing rage and an exquisite anguish, suppurating in the soul for two years, welled up into his sun-washed eyes. He stared across the shortgrass plain in the general direction of Two Rivers, as though he could see the town—and the object of long-nurtured vengeance—across the tan and dusty miles.

Reese looked that way too, but he was visualizing something else entirely.

"I've heard that the town marshal is pretty tough. Been there over a year. A long time for a badgetoter to stay upright in a trail town. But they say that he is mean enough to walk 'em down."

"I don't care how mean or tough he is."

"Well," drawled Reese, "maybe *you* don't. But if I'm the one who kills the cardsharp, then I'm the one that lawman draws down on."

Kane snorted. "You knew the lay of the land before you signed on. Getting cold feet all of a sudden?"

The gunslinger's expression was as murky and unpleasant as mudslime at the bottom of a fouled waterhole.

"Thy will be done, Mr. Kane. Like the Bible-thumpers say at prairie revival. And if the badgetoter gets in my way, well . . ." Reese moved his bony shoulders again. "It's what I do. We all have a reason for being put on this earth. I'm here so that upstanding citizens like you can have that Old Testament eye-for-an-eye and still keep the hands clean." Grinning, he held up one hand, fingers splayed. "But my hands ain't clean."

Kane frowned. He was a prideful man. Proud of all his accomplishments, racked up against heavy odds and the dream-killing whimsy of Fate. Now it occurred to him that there were some things a man had to do that he could not be proud of—in truth, would be ashamed to admit if he were any kind of man at all. But that didn't change the fact that those things sometimes had to be done.

"Go into town tonight, check into The Plainsman. Don't look for me. When the time comes I'll find you."

With those terse instructions he touched the bay with his spurs and cantered off toward the herd, cold to the bone despite the hammer of the sun's heat across his shoulder blades.

Chapter Three

Irish Joe Kempen was one of Two Rivers' full-time deputy marshals. He was also Marshal Brackett's good friend, a circumstance to which, in part, he owed his present employment. One of Brackett's first official acts as the trail town's peace officer had been to send a wire fetching Irish. The latter had been pan-sloshing in a Colorado minefield, but he had abandoned his fruitless flirtation with the mother lode and hauled his freight for Two Rivers without the benefit of second thought, arriving in a timely fashion for the privilege of standing as best man in the wedding. Maris was the best thing to ever happen to Clem Brackett. Irish didn't care what anybody said.

Unlike Brackett, Irish had never worn a star before. The job was long on risks and responsibilities, but Kempen had handled the pressures admirably. And, again unlike his friend, it wasn't as if he didn't know how to live any other way. In his twenty-eight years Irish had wandered all over creation. From iron-road naddie to bullwhacker, from prospector to ranch hand, he had dabbled and drifted. About the only two things he had never been were wanted by the law and settled down. There was no hankering in him to try the first, and he hadn't found the right woman for the second.

A rangy redhead, in some ways Irish Joe resembled the men

who caroused through the saloons and dancehalls on the Texas Side. He wore his trousers tucked into mule-ear boots and a red flannel shirt, the cuffs rolled up over the sleeves of faded-to-pink longhandles. And like the drovers he watched over, he was possessed of a devil-may-care smile and a hair-trigger temper, proud and quick to take offense, with a brash, half-wild glimmer in his shamrock-green eyes and a confident roll to his walk. But he wore no spurs on his boots, and there was hardly a cowboy worth his salt who didn't take secret pleasure in hearing the scrape and jingle of big steel rowels on the scuffed and scarred wooden floors of the boardwalks and bawdy-houses. Spurs were as much a badge of honor for the Texas cowpuncher as the four-pointed piece of polished tin, hooked to his gunbelt, was to Irish. Another thing that set Irish apart was his habit of going about bare-headed. He was this side of vain concerning his auburn curls. A cowboy, on the other hand, always dressed from the top down, and felt as naked as a newborn without his headgear on.

What set Irish apart more than anything else, though, was his stick. While he carried a Colt Lightning revolver on his side, Kempen's weapon of choice was a thirty-inch length of white maple. Round and smooth, it was remarkably sturdy and lightweight. He had fashioned a grip from strips of rawhide and attached a wrist thong through a hole carved in one end. Born and raised on the rough streets of Chicago's Shantytown, Irish retained vivid memories of Shytown constables, who had polished their proficiency with the nightstick to the level of an art. And later in life, as a youngster just striking out on his own into the frontier, he had witnessed firsthand the expertise of railroad bulls with their billy clubs. These still-bright recollections, coupled with the inescapable fact that he was no hand with a sidearm, had led to Kempen's stick. More than a few cowboys spoke of it these days around the campfire or doghouse, and some did so with a flinch.

For the better part of a year Kempen had worked the night shift, coming on at sunset and making his rounds until the early morning hours when the town got empty and quiet, then to retire to the jail to rest with one eye open until dawn. This time of year he rarely took a day off. Many of the herds trailed north in the fall, when September rains nurtured summer-wasted rivers with enough water for those thousands of thirsty beeves. Irish didn't mind the long hours. Clem had his wife to go home to. And Maris, thought Irish admiringly, was as pretty as moonrise on high mountain snow. He, on the other hand, had only his job to occupy the time.

It was not his habit to make regular rounds. Rather, he let instinct guide him. If a trail town lawman was worth his salt he developed a feel for the night as it rollicked through the Texas Side. The night had a life of its own, the action a distinct pulse, and Irish could feel it in his bones. He was part of it. When trouble was about to erupt that pulse quickened, and Irish felt the change and was drawn to it like a hunting animal to fresh spoor.

At about eight o'clock he was moving down the east side of Smoke Street, the main thoroughfare on the Texas Side. Behind him lay the deadline of Main, past which a cowpoke ventured only if he longed to experience the iron amenities of jail. The deadline was an invisible and inviolate wall, separating good and evil in Two Rivers. North of Main, the respectable segment of town was dark and peaceful and sleeping. Down here, though, the action swelled at high tide. The windows and doors blazed with yellow light that fell out onto the rutted hardpack of Smoke and deepened the dangerous shadows. Men yelled and laughed and cursed and drank and gambled. The hitchrails were packed with tethered horses. Cowboys tramped up and down the boardwalks and angled back and forth across the street, desperate to sample the delights of as many of the Smoke Street establishments as they could.

Irish walked with an easy stride through the revelry, quiet and resolute. He did not strive to cast his presence on the consciousness of these men. He did not require them to move out of his way, though like as not they did of their own accord. No, it wasn't his aim to rain on their parade. He liked the wild young Texas drovers and felt that they had earned the right to let loose and howl. It wasn't confrontation that he sought. His purpose was to stop trouble, not start it. If his big fists couldn't deal with the problem, the stick would do the trick. Irish was proud of the fact that he had not yet been forced to kill a man. That was not an itch he felt compelled to scratch, either.

Coming up on the doorway of the Lone Star Dancehall he felt the night's pulse quicken. A heartbeat later there was a shout from within, a girl's screech, and a brief scuffle; then a drover came hurtling backwards through the open doorway, flying past Kempen's nose in a tangle of lanky legs. The cowboy tried to catch himself but lost his balance on the rim of the boardwalk and toppled hard into the street. Irish stood still and watched him. With a strangled growl signaling damaged pride, the Texan pushed to his feet and started a charge aimed at the doorway, shoulders bunched and fists balled up. The sight of Kempen standing there arrested him in midstride. Irish watched the rapid play of strong emotion on the sunburned face as the drover took the measure of a man he had not met until now but had already heard plenty about. There wasn't a dime's worth of difference between Marshal Clem Brackett and the bare-headed Irishman who backed him up when it came to being hard as nails.

As his gaze locked on the stick dangling from Kempen's wrist, the cowboy's body unwound. Irish saw reason wash the wrath out of the boy's face and was glad. The deputy was careful not to portray any challenge in his stance or expression. This he had learned from watching Brackett at work. The veteran of half a dozen such jobs, Clem knew how to move into the stream of trouble and dam up the current of deadly pride, unyielding as stone. But he didn't push back.

The Texan bent to fetch his hat from the dust, whacked it against his leg with a sullen ferocity, and shot one more hard and reckless look in Kempen's direction, but Irish merely turned away to cross the threshold of the Lone Star, thereby letting the cowboy restore at least a portion of dignity at his expense. It didn't cost him anything. The Texan turned away to seek other diversions, his resentment down to a manageable simmer now.

One step into the dancehall and Irish found an obstacle in the person of Sulky, the Lone Star's bouncer. Sulky was a head taller than Kempen and twice as wide. Arms as big around as any other man's thighs were folded across an enormous chest. Sulky was acknowledged to be the biggest man in Two Rivers. His blue-jowled face was split into a grin of wonderful anticipation that wilted as he identified Irish, and the small black eyes beneath the jutting parapet of his bushy brows grew as sad as a bloodhound's. He unfolded his arms and shoved his ham-sized hands as far down into the pockets of his moleskin pants as they would go.

"Doggone it, Irish! Thought for sure and certain that wall-eyed poke would come back for more."

"He's moved on to greener pastures, Sulky."

"You spoiled my fun."

"Did you toss him?"

Sulky shook his head. "Couple of his *amigos* beat me to it. He was getting the bit in his teeth 'cause one of the girls wouldn't run off to Texas with him. Guess them others were inclined to dance with her before she made any long-range plans."

"True love loses out again," grinned Irish. He glanced at the wall to his left, where dozens of shell belts, weighted down with sidearms of every description, dangled from long pegs.

"If he left his iron here I imagine he'll be back."

"You must've scared him something fierce."

"No, Sulky. He wasn't scared. He may be young, but he had seen hell and high water. I'd say he was smarter than you give him credit for being. But then you're so godawful huge you can afford to underestimate 'em."

Sulky shrugged. Nothing pleased him more than a good fracas. Irish had seen him throw drovers around like toys. But he was not a vicious type, really. He just thought of fighting as good clean fun and fine exercise.

"I'll give him some rope if he comes back," promised the bouncer. "As long as he don't persist in that crazy notion about dragging one of the girls back home with him. I wouldn't wish that on any of them. Sherman was right when he said that if he owned Texas and Hell, he'd rent out Texas and live in Hell."

Irish smiled tolerantly. "Ever been to Texas, Sulky?"

"Heavens, no! But I've seen her sons and they are devils every one."

Irish stepped to one side in order to look past Sulky's breadth. The band had just struck up a spirited gallopade—the band consisting of a piano, a fiddle, and an accordian. Two dozen happy cowboys swept as many gaily clad chippies onto the dance floor. Irish felt the floor beneath his feet shudder with the thunder of pounding bootheels, and coyote yells rang through the smoke-wreathed rafters. The percentage girls were game enough, with their far-off eyes and mechanical smiles and hurting feet. The walls were lined with more drovers, as was the long mahogany tended by a trio of hustling barkeeps in whiskey-stained canvas aprons. Irish was familiar with the routine. The band would play for a couple of minutes and then stop for five, long enough for the men to buy drinks for their dance partners. At the Lone Star the girls drank ginger beer, at two bits a glass. Their percentage was half. A woman on ginger beer could go through a squadron of cowboys knocking back unadulterated snakehead. But it was a tough way to make a living, and Irish felt a little sorry for the girls. Maybe, he mused, it wasn't such a poor choice after all when one of them latched on to a man for better or worse. Was the life of a frontier wife harder than this? He knew that Sulky didn't like it when a girl pulled out. Odd as it was, Sulky relished the role of big brother to all the Lone Star doves.

Some of the cowboys not engaged in do-si-do were watching him, wary as mavericks. "I'll be going!" he shouted at Sulky over the din of the music, and Sulky yelled back, "Watch your backside, Joe!" and Irish stepped out into the night.

Standing a moment on the boardwalk, careful not to put himself against the yellow backwash of light coming through the doorway, he drew the night air deep into his lungs. It was brisk and clean, an antidote to the harsh mix of sweat and smoke and sour liquor that pervaded the Lone Star and all the other dens along this street. Turning south, he strolled past the bucket-of-blood saloon owned by Sawdust Sally, and fifty paces farther on came to the corner of The Palace, Clyde Hobart's sourmash mill. He paused at the plate glass window long enough to survey the long, narrow room and ascertain that all was well. The Palace was a less festive scene than the Lone Star. Here the Texans got down to the business of losing their hard-earned wages in games of chance. As usual, a smoky haze hung thick and lazy beneath the high green-tin ceiling. Men were bellied up shin-by-shoulder to the bar, and the deal tables were crowded. A wheel of fortune was spinning like a windmill with a zephyr in its teeth. The faro dealer, Jean Claude, stood out in his canary yellow silk shirt and gold vest, his obsidian hair ashine with a heavy dose of rose oil, his shrewd smile never changing as he cleaned the pockets of the men who were fool enough to "buck the tiger." Right up near the window, the gambler Lee Stanhouse played poker the way an artist worked canvas. His somber black frock coat set off the unhealthy pallor of the skin pulled taut across the fine bones of his melancholy face. He was dealing a hand, sending red-backed pasteboards spinning across the green baize with unerring accuracy. The three range riders who braved his table watched his long articulate fingers speak their mesmerizing language. Irish figured these three would go home poor as Job's turkey.

Someone came around the far corner of The Palace, emerging light-footed from the pitch of the alley, and Irish tensed, until the orange glow from the fired tip of a long-nine illuminated the smooth round face of Clyde Hobart. The saloon owner gave Irish a faintly superior smile that lacked a trace of genuine friendliness.

"Easy, Mr. Kempen. Just out for a stroll."

"Maybe you should put a little more weight in your step," suggested Irish, without rancor.

Hobart's chuckle was deep, mellow and tolerant as he moved closer into the light blazing from his place. He wore a fine blue broadcloth suit and benchmade Middletons polished to a rich luster. He smelled of money and power and French quinine, and he was the man who spoke for the clique that owned the Texas Side concerns.

"I haven't had the opportunity lately to tell you what a fine job we all think you are doing, Mr. Kempen."

Irish always felt uneasy around Hobart, but he never let it show. "That's good to hear," he replied flatly.

"I'm sure Clem rests easy, knowing that the streets are in good hands."

"They're still in his hands, Mr. Hobart. He's still the marshal."

"Naturally. I'm only hoping to convey our confidence in his decision to leave the night shift in your charge. I know Mrs. Brackett is relieved that the marshal takes his responsibilities as a husband and future father so seriously."

Irish saw it clearly now, having learned to read Hobart as a man who had refined a habit of saying one thing and meaning another into art. If nothing else, Irish was a friend who stood steadfast behind Clem Brackett. An undercurrent in Hobart's remark rubbed against the grain and flared dangerously close to the powder keg that was the deputy's temper.

"For a man who never had a good thing to say about him when he was out here keeping the lid on every night," Irish remarked, "you sound like you resent the fact that he left you and yours in my hands."

The hard edge in Kempen's tone took Hobart aback, but he was quick on his feet and the surprise barely showed.

"And very capable hands they are, too. I think you misunderstood me."

"Maybe," allowed Irish, dubious.

"Come on inside, Mr. Kempen. Have one on the house. I've got a crate of honest-to-God Kentucky bourbon just freighted in."

"Don't you think I'd be bad for business?"

"There is never any trouble in my place, so you won't have to exert your authority." Hobart's eyes glanced off Kempen's stick.

"Never? Hmm. Seems like I recollect otherwise."

Hobart's expression turned stony. "That was a long time ago, if you are referring to what I suspect you are. A lot of water under the bridge. And that was before your time. Personally, I feel it unwise to speak of things without firsthand knowledge."

Irish let that polished rebuke run off him like rainwater. Compelled to impress on Hobart the fact that he was not one to tamper with, he bent his head toward the window.

"Stanhouse is back dealing with you, when I would've thought he'd stay clear of Two Rivers. I'd have thought you'd keep him out."

"I won't hold it against him," replied Hobart righteously. "He was not to blame. It was self-defense. I know what I'm talking about. I was there."

"You're a high-minded man, Mr. Hobart," nodded Irish with such superb sincerity that Hobart could not be sure whether sarcasm lingered in the remark. "You'll play fair with a man whether it is bad for business or not."

Hobart's head moved sideways, and his eyes narrowed. "I don't follow."

With a shrug Irish moved on past the saloon owner.

"Guess we'll just hope Texas has a short memory. Good evening."

Chapter Four

Kempen walked down to the end of Smoke and paused to look south, across Kiowa Street, which marked the edge of town, at the long lengths of the C&NW railhouses. On the far side of the tracks were the stockyards, a full square mile of them, already filled with cattle. This close, the air was thick with the smell of them. Down among the dozens of cattle cars lined up on sidings he saw the blaze of a bonfire and dark shapes moving around it. The train crews tended to steer clear of the Texas Side. Generally they did their work and stayed out of trouble. Way off in the inky flats Irish saw pinpoints of lights set well apart: the night camps of the drovers of several more herds, newly arrived. In the morning federal inspectors would ride out and look close for trail fever. Once the herd was certified and sold to one of the many brokers set up in town, the drovers would draw their pay and ride hell bent for election into "Little Texas."

Hearing the clip-clop of a shod horse moving slow, Irish looked left. A moment later the rider came close enough for Kempen to recognize Linus Russell. Most men called him Patch, due to the square of brown leather that covered the empty socket of his left eye. The spotted gray he rode looked as heavy-footed and lackadaisical as an old plow mare. Although Patch was Brackett's other deputy, Irish knew little about him.

Russell wasn't the sort to lower his guard and let people in close. And until a week ago Patch had worked the day shift. Irish couldn't help feeling uncomfortable around the man, and that wasn't good, because from now on they had to rely on one another.

"Nice night," remarked Irish lamely, striving for a camaraderie that wasn't in his heart.

"Getting cold," muttered Patch, slumped in the saddle, shoulders knotted under a shapeless woolen coat. "Don't care for cold nights, myself. Remind me of what I ain't got no more. A man needs a good woman to keep him warm on nights like this."

Irish grimaced. Sometimes Patch managed to infect others with the misery that seemed to cling to his every word and gesture like the ripe stench of something long dead.

Patch glowered up at a sky thick with frost-rimmed stars. "Have a blue norther pass through before much longer," he presaged. "First, a hard rain, with hail the size of eggs, maybe, and then a wind that will turn your blood into ice." His lantern-jawed face was sallow and morose, and his eyes were as cold and distant as the stars as he fastened them on Kempen. "Mark my words. It'll come. You'll see."

"I believe you," said Irish, lacking any better response, and not bothering to point out that the kind of weather Patch foretold always *did* come, sooner or later, this time of year. Patch was forever giving dire warning of things folks already knew to look out for.

"Just come from Yellowtooth," advised Russell, meaning the road that ran parallel to Smoke and to the east. "Seen the marshal's horse tied up in front of Magruder's. What do you think about that?"

"He and Magruder are friends."

"Hardly seems fitting," decided Patch stiffly. "Last I looked the marshal was a married man. And Magruder runs a cathouse."

"It's not a green-shade crib and you know it," sighed Irish, with fresh dislike for Russell's holier-than-thou point of view. "He just boards the percentage girls. He doesn't allow men visitors."

"Except the marshal."

Not for the first time it occurred to Irish that Patch had never been able to loosen up enough to call Brackett by his name. Kempen wondered if perhaps Russell nurtured some hidden resentment toward Clem. After all, Patch had been a deputy in Two Rivers before Clem Brackett had signed on. The town council had passed over Russell when they had lured Brackett away from Broken Bow to take the place of the previous marshal, who had been forcibly retired by a bullet in the back.

Irish said nothing, though, wishing to drop the subject. It was Russell who wanted to worry it until it bled.

"All I'm saying is that on a night like this, or any night, I'd be with my wife. That's why he took over my shift in the first place, wasn't it?"

Irish stiffened, fighting his temper again. The way he saw it, Patch was backstabbing Clem just as Hobart had done earlier, only more bluntly. But Kempen was angered even more by the unnerving doubts Russell's complaints had aroused in his own mind. What *was* Brackett doing, visiting Magruder? Giving into pressure from Maris, Clem had traded shifts with Patch so that he could spend his evenings at home. Irish had seen from the outset that this was a decision fraught with risk. Inevitably some would say that the marshal had lost the grit it took to roam the Texas Side at night. Irish had prepared himself for battle in defense of his friend, yet tonight Brackett wasn't where he was supposed to be. Somehow Irish felt betrayed.

"If you didn't like the arrangement," he snapped testily, "why didn't you speak up at first?"

"What do you mean?"

"You don't strike me as a man keen on being out in the middle of it."

Patch Russell had been resting a 10-gauge sawed-off Davenport across his saddlehorn. Now he lifted it, a sharp and angry motion, to lay it against his right shoulder.

"You think these Texas boys scare me?"

"No," said Irish, disgusted. He had no ironclad evidence for casting aspersions on Russell's backbone, but his instincts warned him not to put his trust in this man, or place his life in his hands. "I think you hate them, Linus. With a hate that burns like rattler spit. I think you blame every single one of them for what happened to you a long spell back."

Patch turned his head to gaze darkly out at the distant night camps.

"Yeah, I hate them," he murmured, his voice thick and trembling. "They are a scourge on this land. They dirty up everything they lay hand on. They're wicked destroyers of all that's good and decent. Their herds waste the earth. I had a wife and a fine strapping boy and a homestead. I busted my back day in and day out to bring forth the fruits of the soil. I was building a dream into a future. And then they came and took it all away."

"Linus, that was a terrible thing. But the men who did it to you paid the price. Besides, they may have been cowboys like the men who pass through here, but that doesn't mean these men are to blame, does it? For the most part the Texas boys are decent enough. They're full of wild juice, sure, but that doesn't make them bad characters."

"They're evil," said Patch with flat conviction, "and I will stand against them until Judgment Day."

He squeezed his knees against the gray's ribcage, and the horse moved listlessly. Irish watched him cross the foot of Smoke Street and vanish into the deep shadow of Kiowa, and wondered why Clem Brackett allowed such a man to stay on. The only thing, Kempen reasoned, that had kept Patch Russell clear of a fatal showdown thus far was a shortage of the guts it would take to vent his hate.

Ill at ease, Irish started to bend his steps down Kiowa to Yellowtooth Road, but faltered and shook his head. No, Clem was over there, and Kempen felt a bothersome inclination to avoid his friend tonight. He turned and went back around onto Smoke, to be met by a gust of cold night wind that slipped right through his clothes and gave him an icy embrace. He clenched his teeth and shuddered violently. All at once the full scope of his loneliness came to him, the barren vista of future years, and he heard Russell's lament about a man's need on such a night as this. An errant thought of Maris ambushed him, and he was ashamed. The wind cut his eyes and made them wet and then was past him, gone howling in the narrow notches between the cattle cars down by the stockyards.

He trudged on, hearing familiar sounds drifting across the street: the tinny tone of pianos, the clink of glass and the clatter of coin in the sourmash mills, the rolling thunder of stomping booted feet as drovers caged the bird in the dancehalls, the rip and roar of lusty male voices laced with the randy lilt of a girl's laughter. And beyond the lights and the raw clapboard were the wide open plains, and he felt the immensity of that silent, magnificent expanse, and his own smallness and inconsequence.

The creak of bat wings caught his attention. Two drovers stumbled out of Sawdust Sally's a hundred yards upstreet. Irish stopped and became a part of the boardwalk shadow. Laughing irrepressibly, like children, the cowboys tried to fight the blind staggers and strap on their gunbelts at the same time. This kindled a keen interest in Irish. A cowboy on the Texas Side had to remember two rules: to stay south of the Main Street deadline and to leave their guns checked until they were ready to ride out of Two Rivers for good. Immediately Irish assumed the responsibility of unseen shepherd. Those boys had committed themselves. If they didn't go he would have to send them on their way.

The brace of range riders shuffled out into the middle of Smoke, and Irish went forward with quick, long strides. But he slowed his pace as he realized, by the way they cast about and from their loud talk, slurred with busthead liquor, that they sought their horses among the multitude lined up at the tie rails.

Still walking, Irish watched as they spied their mounts and, with much foolish hilarity, managed to climb into their saddles. Then one cut loose with a coyote yell that rang against the false fronts of the Smoke Street buildings. The other demonstrated the agility of his wiry cowpony by turning it round and round in a tight circle, raising a veil of dust that was bone-white in the moonlight. Irish felt the skin tighten across his shoulders, and picked up the pace, closing fast, instincts aroused.

A shot rang out. Shouts rose from all points. Windows and doorways quickly filled with figures, and the street grew darker. Bursts of flame erupted above the cowboys as they aimed carelessly at the sky. Irish stepped out into the street and threw a glance behind him in the direction of Smoke's intersection with Kiowa. No sign of Patch Russell. That came as no surprise. Irish allowed himself an ironic smile, squared his shoulders and went on, swinging his stick.

One of the Texans finally spotted the deputy coming up the middle of the street. He saw a man without a hat and without a horse. He failed to see the badge riding low on Kempen's shellbelt, and the stick did not register at all in his whiskey-befuddled brain. In short, he saw someone at whose expense he thought he could have more fun.

So with a wild whoop he raked his big-roweled Chihuahua spurs across the flanks of his horse, and the pony shot forward with a snorting scream, blowing steam out its nostrils. As he came on, the cowboy fired a shot. The bullet kicked up a spray of dirt a reach away from Kempen's left boot. Irish wasn't expecting such stupidity. He jumped involuntarily, and his hand dropped to the butt of his sidegun. "Crazy fool," he muttered, disbelievingly. The next instant found the drover pulling up, drawing back on the reins so hard that his animal's head flew up and back savagely, the hind legs slid out from under, and the rump went down to the hardpack so close that

Irish stood fast in a spray of dirt. The mount recovered to stand next to Kempen, legs atremble. The Texan sat stiffly, staring at the badge he had finally seen.

"My kettle's in the fire," he murmured, stunned by the enormity of his mistake.

"Drop the gun and climb down, mister."

It was bad manners to call a cowboy "mister," but Irish was in no mood to stand on etiquette.

The young drover, his movement ginger, slipped his gun into its holster. "No harm meant. I wasn't shootin' at you. Let me ride on out."

"No deal. Get down or be dragged down."

Kempen's inflexibility offended the drover's sense of fair play.

"You ain't takin' me to jail," he whispered sullenly. "I won't stew in some damned iron cage. *Hiya!*" He laid in his spurs again. This time the horse balked, having endured all the mistreatment it intended to. The cowboy cursed a blue streak. Irish stepped in fast. The stick whistled through the air and caught the rider squarely in the kidney. The Texan let out a strangled yell. Irish grabbed a handful of shirt and gave a tremendous yank. The drover was too awash in agony to catch himself. He came flying out of the saddle, striking the hardpack awkwardly. The horse bolted, and Irish closed in quickly as the Texan, every labored breath a testament to pain, swayed to his feet, filling his hand with the gun at his side once again and turning to find the man who had hurt and humiliated him.

Irish swung the stick again. It clanged against the barrel of the revolver and drove it from the Texan's grasp. Irish put his shoulder into a left cross that connected solidly with the cowboy's face, breaking the nose. The Texan went down, flat on his back. Looking around, Irish spotted the gun in the dust and moved to retrieve it. As he straightened, the drover sat up, a rivulet of dark blood on his petulant chin.

"Gimme my iron," he said, low-down and resentful.

"Sure, I'll give it to you," replied Irish, admiring the man's spunk as his own anger ebbed. "Across the teeth if you don't shut up."

A shout caused Kempen to turn, and he saw the other cowboy whipping his horse forward. With the taste of iron in his mouth, Irish realized that this one was intent on riding him down and rescuing his *compañero*. The deputy felt the weight of the first puncher's hogleg in his hand. But then another horseman appeared, emerging unexpectedly from an alley. It was Patch Russell, his spotted gray moving with uncharacteristic spryness. Irish was saved from having to decide whether to use the weapon. The drover quickly checked his pony as the sawed-off Davenport looked him in the eyes with both barrels.

"I got Dupont double-ought buckshot here," rasped Patch thickly, "and a fierce hankering to splatter Texas blood all over Nebraska dirt."

Irish felt the street freeze still as death in a breathless tension.

"Come on," begged Russell. "You're not gonna back down from a broken old sodbuster, are you?"

Seeing the notion play across the youngster's ruddy features, Irish intervened with a sharp and desperate caveat.

"Don't play the fool, cowboy."

The drover's hot glance flickered in Kempen's direction.

Irish said, "It's a dumb move when you draw on a man who's got the drop on you. That's the way you'll be remembered. Not very flattering."

The cowboy saw the light of reason. Moving slow, he lifted both hands and grabbed hold of his vest high on the chest.

Irish looked at the man sitting nearby in the street.

"Get up and walk with me."

The cowboy complied, his face already swelling badly. Kempen went around to take the other drover's gun from its holster. "Step off," he ordered, and the man swung to the ground. Irish gave Patch an unfriendly look.

"It would've been murder, Linus."

Russell appeared devoid of emotion. "I'd say fair justice."

Irish simply shook his head, feeling sour and empty. The action over, people began to drift away from the doors and windows to resume the night's activities. A moment later a piano player began to bang the ivories. Something drew Kempen's attention to a figure cut in half by shadow on the boardwalk fronting The Palace. The man lounged at the corner of the building, a few strides from the window where Kempen had stood talking to Hobart scarcely more than a half-hour earlier. Irish glimpsed buckskin leggins and the bottom half of a gray duster. He kept his eyes on the figure, his instincts warning him again. But the man put both hands out in front of him, into the light from the window. The hands were empty, the palms turned down, the fingers splayed. And then the man pushed away from the wall and melted into the thick gloom of the nearby alley.

"We goin' to jail?" sulked one of the cowboys.

"Damn straight," snapped Irish, shoving the confiscated guns under his belt. "You gonna press the issue?"

"Just askin'," was the subdued reply.

"Come on, then," said Irish, and led the way up Smoke toward Main, bringing the second Texan's horse. The pair of drovers trudged along in his wake. Patch took up the rear on the gray, a grim and hostile presence.

Chapter Five

Standing at the window, Brackett said, "I'd better get down there."

"What for?" asked Magruder, making his tone casual. "The shooting has stopped. Sounds like the war is over." He brushed ineffectually at the wet spot on the front of his shirt. Having pulled his wheelchair up close to the red-leather wing chair where, a moment before, the marshal had been sprawled, he had been startled by Brackett's quick reaction to the gunfire. Brackett had come out of that chair like a rock out of a slingshot, causing Magruder to slosh bourbon on his shirt. Magruder was astonished that a man could move so reflexively to a sound that, more often than not, froze others in their tracks. But then, he reminded himself, Brackett was no ordinary *hombre*.

Brackett stayed where he was, looking out at the night. "Because it's my job, Mac, and you know it."

"You can't ride the streets twenty-four hours a day. That's why this town shells out to give you a pair of deputies. Besides, don't you think Kempen can handle it? Hell, you're the one who brought that hardfisted Irishman to Two Rivers in the first place."

"He's a good man in a tight spot."

"Then let him do what you picked him for—and what we pay

him for. Jesus, Clem, you're as fidgety as bacon in a hot skillet. You made me spill a dime's worth of Overholt on my good clean shirt. Now you plan to waltz out there and let Kempen know you don't think he can get it done. You got so many friends, I suppose, that you can afford to throw one or two by the wayside without a by-your-leave."

Brackett gave the dark stretch of Yellowtooth Road a final survey, then turned on Magruder with a wry smile breaking beneath the drape of his thick, dark mustache.

"No," he said, his voice a deep, slow drawl, "I don't have *that* many. All the same, I'd like to know the particulars."

Magruder rolled his eyes, dramatizing exasperation.

"Honestly, Clem. I know you. You're so stubborn that you'll fuss like a jaybird over a garden snake until you have your way." He raised his bull voice in a holler fit to bring down the rafters. "*Daybreak!* You lazy heathen! Get your little brown butt in here!"

The door to the downstairs hall opened immediately, and Magruder ruthlessly stifled a grin. He had fully expected Daybreak to be near at hand. She always was, when Brackett was visiting. A willowy young woman, endowed with the build and fragile features of a white girl and the rich, burnished mahogany coloring of her Arapaho mother, she stood meekly a step inside the book-lined study of her father. Magruder noted how her smoky eyes kept flicking across the marshal, only to slide shyly away.

"Clem here has a favor to ask," said Magruder, a twinkle in his eyes. Daybreak's whole attention locked with such eagerness upon him that Brackett shifted his weight uncomfortably.

"Hell, Mac," he growled, embarrassed. "I'll go see for my own damn self."

"Sit down, you stubborn so-and-so. My daughter is always happy to do a favor for a friend. Daybreak, you heard the gunplay? Why don't you go on out and find out what happened? Do it quietly."

"Yes, Father."

As she left the room, Brackett couldn't help but notice what a fine figure she cut in her plain yellow percale dress, and how her long black hair, brushed out, gleamed in the lamplight. Magruder, on the other hand, took note of her bare feet and shook his head resignedly as she shut the door softly behind her.

"Can't seem to keep that child in shoes, Clem."

"How can you send her out into the night like that?" asked Brackett, sharp and accusatory. "We're well to the south of Main, and she can't expect to get the kind of respect those drovers will show a full-blood white woman."

Magruder snorted and took an appreciative sip of the bourbon remaining in his glass.

"The Lord help those gallop-and-gunshot boys if they fool with her. She can be a handful of hellcat, just like her mother was." With the dexterity of many years' practice, Magruder spun his creaking wooden wheelchair and rolled to the cluster of crystal decanters on a tall, mirrored sideboard. "How about another long pour of this high-class bobwire extract, boy?"

"I'll pass, thanks all the same."

Pouring for himself, Magruder watched Brackett in the mirror as Clem half-turned his head toward the window, listening to the muted symphony of sounds that "Little Texas" played every night. Brackett was in tune with that wild music. He had been a part of the action for so long, with such intensity, that it had become second nature to him, and he felt now like a fish out of water.

The old Regulator on the wall between the ranks of laden bookshelves clanked out the hour. Magruder was still watching as Brackett looked at the time, and saw the shadow of guilt pass over the marshal's face.

"Nine o'clock, and all's well," intoned Magruder, rolling back across the room. The shotglass, full again, rested in a notch carved into the rosewood armrest of the wheelchair. Magruder moved the contraption with such smooth strength across the polished oak floor that the amber liquor barely stirred. Magruder's chest and shoulders were thick with layers of muscle. He could transport himself on level ground almost as fast as a man could run full tilt. But his legs, long-unused, had wasted away to sticks. He kept them covered with a red and black Indian blanket. His longish hair was silver-white, like the winter coat of a northern timber wolf. His beard was neatly trimmed and full, with a dark streak at the chin. Small red veins laced beneath his piercing eyes and across the bridge of his nose.

"Is it?" asked Brackett tersely.

His resonant voice imbued with a mesmerizing lilt, Magruder recited: "When in disgrace with fortune and men's eyes, / I all alone beweep my outcast state / And trouble deaf Heaven with my bootless cries / And look upon myself and curse my fate, / Wishing me like to one more rich in hope, / Featured like him, like him with friends possess'd, / Desiring this man's art and that man's scope, / With what I most enjoy contented least— / Yet in these thoughts myself almost despising, / Haply I think on thee, and then my state, / Like to the lark at break of day arising / From sullen earth, sings hymns at Heaven's gate."

Brackett stared for a moment at Magruder, astonished.

"You're a strange one, Mac. Mountain man turned man of letters."

"Shakespeare. Sonnet 29, if my memory serves. A man can be a lot of things in a single lifetime. Of course, in my case, there was no alternative, but . . ." Magruder heaved a deep sigh and looked around the room, content in its warmth of dark rich wood and fine hand-tooled leather. "A body has to make the most. You should take the time to read a little, Clem. It's good for you. Take some of these books with you. Lord knows, I have plenty and to spare. All the great captains of literature, you can find them here. Why, I've probably got more books in this room than you could find in all the rest of Nebraska. Poe, Hawthorne, Melville, Thackeray, Byron, Dickens. They used themselves up putting life down on paper, so that others could stand back a ways and watch how it flows and maybe figure out a better way to deal with the rough water ahead of them."

"You're getting long-winded in your old age," smiled Brackett. The tension had drained out of him. That tended to happen when he came into this room and visited this man. He eased his long frame back into the chair. Not for the first time it occurred to Magruder that Brackett moved like a man whose old wounds were sore and stiff. Until he smelled trouble. Then he struck like lightning. Quick and hot and dangerous.

Brackett reached into the pocket of his white muslin shirt and took out a roll of wheat-straw cigarette papers, then delved into a side pocket of his long black coat for the pouch of Lone Jack. The coat fell away and Magruder saw the leather edge of the shoulder rig that held a Porterhouse .37 under the marshal's right arm. Brackett called it his "insurance"; he wore a more traditional weapon, a .44 Remington, on his hip.

"Mind if I smoke?" asked Brackett. Magruder didn't bother to answer. It was an idle question, a ritual of manners, for Brackett knew very well that he did not mind.

Methodically rolling a smoke, Brackett said, "I reckon I know what you are telling me. Problem is, I don't know any other way. I've made my living behind a tin star since I was a wet-behind-the-ears yokel straight out of the cornfields. Knew from the start that my hand did not fit a middle-buster. Old Blue Mitchell was the sheriff of Elkhorn, Missouri, at the time." One side of Brackett's mouth curled. "Old Blue. Carried a damned Hawkens and always had the smell of corn liquor to him. When I went up to him and told him I wanted to be his deputy Old Blue asked me how tough I was. I told him tough enough. So he said, 'We will find out the gospel truth on that subject' and punched me in the face. I laid into him then, harder than a July hound goes after fleas. Didn't let up until I realized he was laughing. Spitting blood and laughing at the same time, like he was fixing to split at the seams. I have never been more proud than when he put that star on my suspenders."

"You looked pretty proud when you said 'I do' in the church."

"Yeah," grunted Brackett.

"You're still proud," said Magruder bluntly, "which is the very reason much of Two Rivers has turned a cold shoulder towards you. You ride the streets like you own them, and I believe that you think that is the case, deep down. I mean, most trail town lawmen *walk* their rounds. But you sit tall on that black-legged Kentucky thoroughbred of yours and go right down the middle of the road, like you care less what comes at you because you know you can handle it. And you can. It's not bravado. That's the worst part of it, for them. They're afraid of you. And it goes against the grain when they back down from what scares them."

Brackett lazily scraped a match to life on the heel of his spurless boot.

"They shouldn't be afraid of me. I don't haze them unless they step out of line."

"It's not just the Texans. What about the people who live in this town? Why should you worry about the drovers? If they have trouble for you they'll give it to you face-to-face. It's the men who run this town that you need to be extra cautious of. They weren't prepared for the kind of man you are when they hired you."

"What kind of man is that?"

"One who casts his own shadow. One who doesn't let others interpret what the law is going to be. Your problem is you won't take sides. You won't run Two Rivers the way the respectable folk want it run. And you won't give as much slack as Hobart and the rest of them on the Texas Side would like."

"You can't please everybody," said Brackett coldly.

"You don't even try."

"The merchants forget what side their bread is buttered on. Without the cattle trade this town would dry up and blow away like dead sage. They want the business but they don't want

50

what comes with it. They have yet to learn that you must take the bad with the good."

"Neither have you. And you're wrong in one regard, boy. You have been looking for trouble up and down Smoke Street for so long that you have missed what's been happening all around. This country is filling up. The trains haul the cattle east and come back filled from woodcar to caboose with homesteaders. More and more, these folks are turning out to be the butter on the merchant's bread. I think it is just now dawning on them."

Brackett's moody gray eyes were narrowed behind the quirling smoke.

"So I should cast my lot with the uptown bunch, is that what you're saying? Clean out the Texas Side? Why, for one thing, I'd put you out of business, Mac."

Magruder grinned. "I told you before. I can roll with the flow."

"If I was their man I wouldn't be able to shoot the breeze with you anymore. They wouldn't permit it."

"Clem, you're just shortsighted, and that's plain. I don't expect you to be anyone's man but your own. You're not made that way. What I am trying to hammer through that thick skull of yours is that times they are a-changing. It won't be too much longer and this town will see that it doesn't have to tolerate the wild Texas drover in order to survive. So you ought to start thinking about your own tomorrows. That will be difficult for a fella who has dedicated his life to just trying to stay alive from one sunrise to the next. But you've already taken the first step. You got yourself hitched to a fine woman. And she's going to make you into a proud father one day soon. I remember that you told me you didn't know what you were doing when you got married. That's the way it is, sometimes. That's common sense leading us by the nose down the right road. That's why you're trying to wean yourself from that action out there."

"It's not my idea," protested Brackett. "I do it for Maris.

She's been after me long enough."

"That's the thing about women," said Magruder earnestly, shaking his head in solemn awe. "They see the future a lot more clearly than men do. You're not ready to admit it, but in your heart you realize that it is the right thing to do."

"So why am I here?"

"Because it is a hard thing to do, also."

Brackett breathed out through his nostrils, long and slow. Then he rose and returned to the window, lifted it open, and flicked his spent cigarette out. Bracing himself against the windowsill he saw the spray of orange embers as it struck the hardpack of the road beyond the veranda rail. He let the night fill his senses with its intoxicating presence.

"You're right," he confessed. "It is hard. My work has a strong pull on me. The feelings I get out there in the street are so strong that the rest of my life seems . . . tasteless by comparison." He made a throwaway gesture. He did not have much of a way with words and sensed that he was doing a pretty poor job of expressing his sentiments.

"Listen to your wife, Clem," advised Magruder, dejection creeping into his voice. "She knows what is best for you. I believe that a person must give up some pleasures in order to have others. You just can't have it all. That is the tragedy of life, if you don't accept it. If you really want a wife and a family and a future you must be rid of the old ways. That's the decision you've got to make, and soon. You can't keep sitting on the fence like a damned meadowlark. And the old ways, it pains me to say, include me."

Brackett turned, incredulous. "That's a steep price," he said bitterly. "You've become a good friend, Mac. One I can talk to. One who listens and who knows what I am trying to say. Everyone needs such a friend."

"When Maris becomes that kind of friend to you, you'll have got it make."

Magruder pivoted the wheelchair to set a course for the sideboard again. He was halfway there when a light rapping sounded and Daybreak slipped into the room like a dream into sleep. Her hungry eyes found nourishment in the sight of Brackett. Her bare feet were covered with the dry dust of the street. She felt Brackett's anxiety and was quick to assuage it.

"Two cowboys made trouble. Your friend has them in jail now. No one was hurt."

Brackett smiled, much relieved. "Thanks, Daybreak, that eases my mind."

Magruder saw the adoring fever in his winsome daughter's expression and turned his chair sharply to face Brackett.

"Clem," he said sternly, "it is past time you got home to your wife. That's where you belong. If you don't realize that pretty damned soon we're all going to wind up in a heap of pain."

Perplexed and stung by Magruder's bluntness, Brackett gathered up his hat. "Thanks for the company and the counsel, Mac. I'll be seeing you."

After the door had closed behind the marshal, Magruder muttered, "Goodbye." As he made for the sideboard something pulled savagely at his heart, for he heard Daybreak slip to the window to watch Brackett ride away.

Chapter Six

Brackett awoke as the first smoky light of the new day crept through the bedroom window. It was cold, that brisk clean and unrelenting cold of winter stealing over the open plains, and yet he was as cozy warm as a man could be, lying beneath the quilted countermane between the crisp percale sheets, his wife beside him. Listening a moment to her breathing, he concluded that she was still sound asleep. The feel of her body against his was a beguiling comfort. In such circumstances a man could own a rare contentment and could drift into believing that all was right with his world.

Moving stealthily to avoid waking her, he slipped his long legs out from under the covers and sat a moment on the edge of the four-poster. Poised there in his long johns, he glanced back over his shoulder and studied Maris's face. Her hair, the color of cornsilk streaked with auburn, was fanned out across the swansdown pillow. Her lips were slightly parted. He fought the urge to lie down again and put his arms around her, press her body—so firm in some places, so pliant in others—against his, smell the sweet breath coming gently out of that lovely mouth with its delicately curved upper lip.

It was too easy, he decided, for a man to grow dependent on a woman's presence. The memory of cold and lonesome nights was one memory that would not fade; it haunted a man into weakness. When Maris had consented to be his bride Brackett had believed himself one of the luckiest men walking the earth. Now he wondered. The way she had brought a change in him had been so subtle and slow that he had not heard it coming.

That change was most obvious to him in the way he approached his work. Before Maris he had waded straight into trouble without a second thought, putting his life on the line without hesitation. He held nothing back and dared everything, because he had felt that there was nothing to lose. Nothing but cold and lonesome nights. Because of this there had been no stopping him. He took on all comers with a half-crazy little smile and a rush of exhilaration, heedless of consequences, unmindful of tomorrow and living for the moment. And other men feared him, for they saw no chink in his armor, not the slightest weakness to turn to their advantage.

And then, Maris. Without realizing it she had crippled him, and he had let it happen. For the first time in his life, in the heat of the moment when tempers ran high and the good fight turned into something brutal and grim, he had been blindsided by the thought of Maris, of all that he had to lose if the tables turned on him, and he had been almost completely unnerved. Old Blue had said that a man was like a sack filled with sand. The sand was courage. Run up hard against the sharp cutting edge of perilous work enough times and the sack ripped open somewhere and the sand began to trickle out. Sometimes in a sudden rush, but usually just a trickle. The end result was the same, however. Brackett had learned early on that Old Blue had been right on the mark with his observation. Clem had seen it happen to his old friend and mentor. Shot to pieces by Blackface Charley Newton, Old Blue had knocked on death's door. Even though he survived, he had come back a different man. It got to the point where Brackett concluded Old Blue would have been better off with his toes permanently curled. The four slugs of lead Blackface Charley had put into Blue had ripped open Mitchell's sack, and all the sand had poured out.

Blue got old overnight, and took to shaking violently at the sound of gunfire.

Of late Brackett had begun to suspect that his own sack had been torn. Not by bullets, as in Old Blue's case, but by his need for the warmth and contentment afforded by the love of a woman.

Wincing at the creak of bed slats, he got up and crossed the small room to his clothes, draped messily across a ladderback chair. One leg in his trousers, he froze and watched breathlessly as Maris stirred beneath the covers. A drowzy moan escaped her, as though deep in her subconscious his drawing away saddened her. Brackett's heart tightened in his chest. He put on his shirt and socks, grabbed up his boots, coat, and gun rigs, then slipped out like a thief.

Their house was a modest whitewashed clapboard on the eastern rim of town, a four-room dogtrot under a brace of sycamores on the road to Kearney. There was a scattering of other houses out this far, including the schoolhouse. His teeth chattered as his jaws locked against the raw bite of the morning. Breath clouding like quirling smoke, he looked left down the length of the open dogtrot as he pulled on his boots, across the road and the stretch of buffalo grass at the line of willows that marked the silver shallows of the South Platte. Beyond the river were the great Texas herds. Beefsteak bound for eastern slaughterhouses. He felt the proximity of the trail crews. Only recently had he begun to consider the drovers a threat. Once he had liked and respected them. Once, but no more.

Finger joints stiff with cold, he strapped the Remington to his hip and fixed the shoulder harness for his Porterhouse .37 into place. He contemplated stepping across into the kitchen to fire up the cannonball stove and brew a pot of strong Arbuckle coffee. But he did not relish the idea of being around when Maris got up. Last night, leaving his horse at Eli's Livery, as was his custom, he had trudged home, the distance of an arrow's flight, to find Maris waiting for him at the kitchen table with a blanket about her shoulders, the rustle of red-hot embers in the stove, and something just as hot in her blue eyes.

"I heard gunfire," she had said. "Some time ago. I was worried."

"No call to be. It's not my shift anymore. I expect Irish handled it."

"No, it's not your shift anymore. But you would like it to be."

He had stood there, his back pressed against the inside of the door, the air between them brittle with wounded feelings, and he was defensive, like a man caught red-handed in the middle of a transgression.

"That's no secret," he had replied, too weary of his dilemma to be anything but brutally frank.

"Then go back to it, if it makes you happy."

"No."

"You're such a stubborn man."

"It's too late."

"What does that mean? Too late for what? You don't make any sense sometimes, Clem Brackett."

Now, he shrugged on his coat and walked out of the dogtrot, across the porch and into the street and the brightening day. The creak and clatter of a spring wagon made him look left. Framed against a horizon aflame with the vivid pink and orange of sunrise, a homesteader wrapped in a blanket coat touched the brim of his hat as he went by and clucked at the pair of heavy dray horses in the traces. Brackett watched him pass with sharp curiosity, harking back to Magruder's remarks the evening before. Maybe Mac was right. Perhaps that man in the wagon box *was* the future, or part of it, a drop in the honest and hardworking tide that was destined to wash away the wild and wicked excesses of the Texas Side. The earth seemed to shift under Brackett's feet as he bent his steps toward Eli's Livery, walking in the wake of the wagon and watching it pull gradually away from him.

He turned off the road and through the tall open doors of the livery barn. Another set of doors at the far end of the carriageway was open, and from the smitty beyond he heard the clang of iron. It was still half-dark in here, as though a portion of the night had been trapped inside these walls. A single kerosene lamp burned, throwing a light like liquid gold down the carriageway. In a stall to Brackett's left his handsome Kentucky-bloodlined sorrel whickered softly at his nearness. Brackett moved on toward the rear of the barn, his footfalls softened by straw. The aroma of horse, leather, and manure rose strong into his nostrils. Passing a buggy with one of its wheels gone and the naked axle resting on a stout wooden sawhorse, he paused for a moment to admire a rimfire saddle thrown over an adzed log. There was some fine hand-tooling on skirt, fenders, and cantle. Brackett passed on through the rear doors. Eli Kesserling, as hard and brown as the ground upon which he stood, looked up from stoking his forge, then came out from under the ramada, wiping blunt, scarred hands on a leather apron.

"You're early, Marshal," he said severely. Eli was as stolid and reliable as a Swiss-made timepiece, and reliability was what he looked for in others. "I usually saddle your horse after I've got my fire going."

Brackett said, "That's all right. I can wait." He did not offer to saddle his own horse. That would have offended Eli, for it was a daily task included in the price Brackett had been paying for a year now.

"No," gruffed Eli. "I'll take care of you, now that you're here."

Brackett smiled, following Eli back into the barn. He was accustomed to Kesserling's sandpaper disposition. Eli always balked at being rushed out of his routine, but when the squalling was done he could be counted on to do the job.

The liveryman stepped up into the tack room, and when he emerged with Brackett's saddle, blanket and curb-bit bridle he saw the marshal idly studying the rimfire.

"Newcomer. Rides that dun mare over yonder. The one

with the roached mane."

Brackett nodded, only mildly interested. "Rancher? Stock buyer?"

"Well, he said he was boarding at The Plainsman, so he isn't a hole-in-the-pocket saddle bum," replied Eli, lugging the gear up the carriageway with Brackett in tow. "But if you want my honest opinion, he's a hired gun."

"What makes you think so?" asked Brackett, his interest on the rise.

Setting down the gear, Eli went into the stall to fetch the sorrel.

"I didn't just roll into town on the tailgate of a prairie schooner, Marshal. I've seen pistolmen in my time. They all got that same half-crazy look, like you see in the eyes of a rabid dog. An I-don't-give-a-damn look. You see it in a man when he cares so little for living that it comes easy, the taking of life."

"Think I'll have a look at his horse," remarked Brackett.

"Be my guest."

When he came back Eli was giving the latigo of the centerfire saddle, now on the sorrel's back, a final tug or two to snug the knot over the front rigging ring. Brackett's brow was furrowed.

"That dun wears a triangle brand. I don't recognize it."

Eli rubbed a hand over his face. "Seem to recollect that a herd came in a couple years ago from a spread called the Triangle. Might be the same mark. Might not."

"Couple of years ago," echoed Brackett. "Before my time. But you say this man was no cowboy."

"I can give an ironclad guarantee on that, Marshal. He wouldn't know an honest day's work if it bit him on the rump."

Brackett shrugged it off. Fitting boot to stirrup, he swung aboard the sorrel.

Eli asked, "How's the missus?"

He had taken a shine to Maris. On occasion she would bring him macaroon cookies, which he had a taste for. She had told Brackett that she sometimes felt sorry for Kesserling, as his wife of thirty-odd years had passed away the previous winter.

Brackett felt guilt stab at him. Last night he had wronged her and they had quarreled. This morning he was running away. The woman who had once been his personal glory had become a subject he did not care to discuss.

"Fine," he said tautly, and steered the responsive horse out into the road, turning right, into Two Rivers.

Chapter Seven

The road to Kearney became Main Street, and down this Brackett rode. He stayed in the middle of the wide thoroughfare, on the "deadline" that separated respectable from disreputable. The sun breached the horizon as he neared the center of town, throwing the long shadow of horse and rider across the ruts in front of them. The homesteader's wagon was parked in front of Leon McKaskle's general store. McKaskle was spokesman and leader of the town's merchants, just as Clyde Hobart, owner of The Palace, stood for the men—and women—who ran the Texas Side. Brackett guessed that the farmer had come to town to buy supplies, and Magruder's words came clear and complete to his mind once more. Until recently McKaskle had been totally dependent on the Texas cowboy for his livelihood. His "shebang" on the south side of Main had been accessible to the drover and carried many of the items that were necessary to the cow trade: hats, boots, spurs, jeans, longhandles, belts, gloves, tobacco, ammunition, rifles and sidearms, tack and rope, dry salt pork, sardines, crackers, canned tomatoes, dried prunes, and other staples of the cowboy's diet.

Pensive, Brackett thought, *Maybe I have had blinders on.* It was simple ciphering, really. The more farmers who brought their trade to Two Rivers, the less the merchants were pressured to cater to the cowpunchers and the less they would feel it incumbent upon them to tolerate Little Texas. And if they pushed out the saloonkeepers and the dancehall girls and the gamblers and the highbinders and all the other undesirables, they would eventually wake to the day when they no longer required the services of a lawman who was known to ride roughshod. Having only recently taken to considering his future, Brackett looked upon it now and saw that it was bleak.

Passing The Plainsman, Brackett was wrapped up in his own thoughts. He did not think about the nameless gunman who, according to Eli Kesserling, currently roomed there. He did not even give the hotel a glance, though it was the only three-story structure in Two Rivers, an impressive edifice with boardwalk and balcony on two sides, standing at the corner of Main and Fremont. The boardwalk was lined with benches and barrel chairs, the uprights adorned with the antlers of deer and antelope.

Brackett was busy worrying about his good friend Magruder. Mac would be included in the list of the unforgiven when the day of reckoning came. Magruder had been one of Two Rivers' first citizens, but he had built his house south of the road that eventually became Main. As Little Texas flourished he had taken to boarding the girls who made their living in the dancehalls. Brackett realized that it would not be news to Magruder that he was some sort of social pariah. He had never been included when the invitations went out for an uptown lawn party. A mountain man who had lived as wild as a grizzly in the high country, who had never had cause to speak his native tongue except at annual rendezvous, and who had roamed the wide-open frontier before it had become burdened with the fetters of civilization, Magruder had taken to his hot roll an Arapaho woman cast out by her people. Daybreak's mother. A woman who had borne the mark of Cain, so to speak, the "dirty nose" sign that branded her as unfaithful to her husband. It was the Arapaho way, the application of a sharp knife, a permanent disfigurement. Magruder, mused Brackett, was a big man with a big heart. He was forever partial to strays. The woman, Mac had said, had had a lot in common with Hester in Hawthorne's *The Scarlet Letter*. By taking in an outcast, Magruder had become an outcast himself, a squaw man whose company was not easily tolerated by proper folk.

As he came up on the jail, Brackett reached the conclusion that, no matter how things changed, Magruder would survive. Some men just laughed and got back up when life knocked them down. Clem wondered if he was one of those men.

There were two horses at the tie rail fronting the jail, one a good-looking Palouse, both wearing double-girthed Texas saddles. Swinging down to tether the sorrel alongside, Brackett automatically checked the flank brand. The mark was an R and a D connected, with the R reversed. A voice raised in righteous anger drifted through the brick walls of the building and into the street. Brackett flexed his shoulders and walked on into trouble.

A wiry little man wearing a gray goatee and a luxuriant mustache drooping to his jawline was pacing the office. Brackett's entrance cut his tirade short, and he drew up to cast a belligerent eye upon the newcomer. Irish was sitting behind the kneehole desk, his feet propped up and his hands locked behind his head, an unruffled expression on his face. That look, Brackett knew, was designed to aggravate.

"You'd be the honcho of this two-bit outfit," barked the agitated stranger.

"I'm Brackett."

"And I am Colonel Riley Davis."

Closing the heavy-beamed door, Brackett appeared unimpressed. "You say that like it should mean something to me."

Davis lifted an arrogant brow. "It will if I don't get what I came for."

Brackett went to the woodburner in the corner. He could feel the heat from the blackened iron, and saw the steam rising from the blue enameled coffeepot. Taking his mug down from a wall peg, he poured himself some java, feeling Riley Davis's gaze boring in between his shoulder blades.

"And what is that?" he asked, although he had drawn his own conclusions.

"You've got two of my hands in your jail. I want them out."

Brackett turned and leaned against a wall littered with wanted posters. He glanced at Kempen.

"What happened?"

"The colonel's boys drank too much forty-rod last night. They started shooting up the street."

"They meant no harm," argued Davis. "They were letting off steam, that's all. You must give these men some elbow room. They work hard and so they play hard. That's what the Texas Side is for."

"They tried to ride me down," said Irish, without rancor. "One of them took a potshot at me."

Davis looked like he wanted to try that himself.

"I find that hard to believe."

"So you have said, more than once. And so did I, as a matter of fact."

Davis eyed Irish as he would look at something stuck to a bootscraper.

"They probably didn't take you for the law. You look more like a lumberjack, or a saloon bouncer."

"They discharged their firearms within the town limits. So I brought them to lockup."

"Fine," barked Davis. "Now let them out."

Irish looked over at Brackett. Davis did likewise. Brackett sipped his coffee.

"I want my boys out of there now or I'll bring my whole crew in here and break 'em out," threatened Davis.

"Give 'em hell, Colonel!" whooped one of the jailbirds. Brackett glanced at the door leading back to the cells.

"Try that," he said softly, "and you'll end up in there with them."

Davis snorted. "You stupid tin star."

Something darkened Brackett's features. His voice dropped

into a deep whisper. "That's a creditable job of sweet-talking, Colonel."

Davis tried to change horses in midstream. "Look. Nobody got hurt. What are you trying to prove?"

"Nothing. We're just doing a job. You'll be short two *hombres* when you go home, unless you want to pay their fine."

"Oh, yes. The fine." Davis smirked. "These boys go through a hundred days of unadulterated hell and get paid a dollar a day to do it. They throw most if not all of it away on bad whiskey, crooked games, and soiled doves. But that's not enough. You look for any excuse to lock them up so that you can rifle their pockets, or mine, for more. This is a greedy, miserable town."

"The fine," said Brackett flatly, "is fifty dollars. A head."

Some of the color faded in the bantam rancher's cheeks. "That rate is steep."

"The fines are set by town ordinance. It is expensive around here, assaulting peace officers."

Resentful, Davis extracted a wallet from the inside pocket of his corduroy coat. As he counted out the money, slapping greenbacks on the desk, Irish got up, took the cell keys from a drawer and went to fetch the prisoners.

"We're not inclined to stand as targets for gunhappy cowpunchers," Brackett told Davis. "You make sure your men remember that, or next time we may end up burying them."

The sullen cowboys shuffled out, pallid and red-eyed. Irish handed them their shellbelts.

Brackett said, "Don't put those on until you're out of Two Rivers. You two aren't welcome in this town anymore."

"You've got a pony over at Doan's Stable," said Irish to one of the drovers. "The other dusted out before we could catch him up. I believe that's the one I saw you leading as you rode in, Colonel."

"It came to camp. That's how I knew my men had been locked up." Davis looked at his cowboys and nodded curtly at the door. The pair trooped out into the morning's brightness. The colonel paused at the threshold, his boys stumbling blindly beyond him on the boardwalk. He turned a vindictive smile on Brackett.

"You don't have to worry about my boys in your town anymore, Marshal. I won't do business in Two Rivers from now on. There are half a dozen other railheads that would want my trade. And I'm not just breaking my elbow when I say that; where I come from, I'm a man that other men listen to. I'll spread the word and the herds will go elsewhere. You hold too tight a rein, lawman. One day you'll look up and Two Rivers will be turning slowly in the breeze. You can bank on that." He went out, slamming the door, self-satisfied.

Brackett said, "I've heard that tune before."

"Well," said Irish wryly, "I guess you can't please everybody all the time."

Brackett folded up the fine and stuck it in a pocket. "Go home, I'll deliver this to McKaskle." The merchant handled the keys to the town's coffers.

"Before you go there's something we need to talk about."

Brackett headed for the door. "I haven't had breakfast or a shave. It can wait."

"No, it can't."

Kempen's iron insistence surprised Brackett and he pulled up.

"It's about Russell," said Irish.

"What about him?"

Irish took his time, trying to pick his words with care.

"Last night he did his level best to prod one of those drovers into gunplay. His hate is eating him raw, Clem. It wasn't so bad when he worked the day shift. He didn't often get an excuse. But out there at night, you know, there are a hundred excuses. All he has to do is pick one."

"Not like you to talk behind a man's back," commented Brackett, in no mood for more to worry about.

Irish reddened, taking offense. "It's just fair warning."

"You don't like working with him."

"I don't know that I can count on him. Only thing that has

kept it from happening so far is that he has to have the drop on them before he'll try it."

"Do you know what you're saying?" asked Brackett, incredulous. "You're making Patch out to be a coward."

"I'm just telling you," said Kempen stiffly.

"Well," said Brackett, bitter, seeing a wall of hard feeling rise up between the two of them. There were times, he reflected, with some self-pity, when every which way a man turned he watched the things he had come to rely on transform into deceptions. It happened when he forgot that all he could really count on was himself. "If you don't like the setup, Joe, you don't have to stick."

Irish nodded slowly. "I've been thinking about it, Clem. I'll let you know."

Brackett spun on his heel and left.

Chapter Eight

Two Rivers was a strange new world to Carson Kane. Riding in stirrup-to-stirrup with his father his neck got to hurting after a spell, since he kept gaping this way and that at the sights. Long removed from civilization, he felt awkwardly conspicuous. He had brushed out his clothes, washed his face, shaved his cheeks, and combed his tangled hair into some semblance of order, yet still he felt like a wild man and half-expected to be stared at. But the townfolk paid no mind.

They circled the stockyards first, a brownish sea of bawling hide. Carson had never seen so much beef in one place. Before they could get across the tracks, the westbound run of the Chicago & North Western Railroad rolled in. A whistle pierced the frosty air and turned their horses skittish. They sat on their dervish mounts as the Jupiter locomotive chugged by, a black monster fashioned from iron and brass and steam with a red cowcatcher up front. The engineer in his black and white overalls threw the throttle lever and turned the valve cutoffs. With a mighty hiss the air pressure escaped the drive cylinders and the train slowed. Then a godawful mechanical clamor rose up as the brakeman laid hold of the Johnson bar. The train came to a grinding halt alongside the long station platform. Tyler forced his bay gelding up and over the graded iron road, and Carson followed suit. He saw a swarm of people offloading: men in flat-brimmed hats and linsey-woolsey shirts under shapeless woolen coats, with flat-heeled, square-toed boots on their feet, the women in austere gingham and bonnets, a passel of children.

"What's going on, Pa?" he asked. "Who are those people?"

"Sodbusters," said Tyler full of disdain, unwilling to even look that way. "Used to be they came by wagon. Some still do. But now that the trains run this far, many of 'em sell out and travel light, their pockets full of grubstake and their eyes set on a homestead." Disgusted, Tyler shook his head. "At least before the railroads they just trickled out here. Now it's a goddamn rushing river. Some call it progress. I say it's a crying shame. They ruin the range, boy. Turn the grass over with their damned middle busters. And they string up the wire. I'd like to shoot the sonuvabitch who invented that stuff."

"Who are the men going out to meet them, dressed up to the nines?"

"Land agents." Obviously Tyler cared as little for them as he did the farmers. "The whole lot oughta stretch hemp, if you ask me."

Carson had just crossed so much wide-open space the past three months that he could not believe there wasn't enough room for every living soul on earth. But he was smart enough to keep that opinion to himself.

They went on up Smoke Street, heading for Main. After all he had heard concerning the Texas Side, Carson was sorely disappointed. The saloons and dancehalls, shut down now, looked dingy and unappealing in the raw morning light. Hardly a soul stirred in Little Texas. Carson could scarcely believe that this was the place that fulfilled a cowboy's wildest dreams.

Coming to Main, a wide river of wheel-creased dust, they turned their ponies to the right and went along a block, then angled to the tie rails fronting the biggest building Carson's young eyes had ever beheld. A sign as large as the bed of a buckboard indicated that this was The Plainsman. They had to cross to the high side of Main to get to it, and having heard of the infamous deadline, Carson got a funny nervous feeling in the pit of his stomach. Most of the Triangle cowboys had pushed a herd to railhead before, and they spoke of a trail town deadline like it was the edge of the world. As though passing over it was as foolhardy as leaping into a rattlesnake pit. To Carson's surprise, no one raised a ruckus. He decided that this had to be because no one would mistake Tyler Kane for a raw-edged, thirty-dollar-a-month cowpuncher. He was clearly here to conduct business, and his kind of business was this town's lifeblood.

Swinging down, father and son hitched their horses and climbed up onto the boardwalk. A pair of townsmen in broadcloth and derbies emerged from the doors of the hotel, touched the brims of their funny-looking hats and moved out of the way. When they looked at him Carson could see, with a burst of pride in his chest, that their eyes contained healthy respect, and suddenly Carson knew why the cowboy was convinced that no man was his better. All the hardships of the trail immediately became wonderful things to have under the belt. Carson's ego swelled.

They entered the lobby, and while Carson drank in the sight of the mirrored pillars and the crystal chandelier and the green carpet with its enormous gold sunburst design, Tyler consulted the tall old Giscard clock over in one corner. He said, "Let's go see what food tastes like when Banjo ain't trying to cook it," and led Carson into the adjoining dining room.

Sitting at a table draped with a blue and white linen cloth, by a window framed with rich green velvet curtains, they were visited by a young woman with a heart-shaped face and sleepy eyes and mousey brown hair. Tyler ordered coffee and doubles on eggs, ham, and biscuits. Carson said, "Same for me," and the girl gave him an odd look because he was gawking at her. He had not been this close to a woman near his own age for a long, long time. It stirred something inside that bothered him as fiercely as a proud saddle sore.

"I guess I'll be coming back into town tonight," he said,

watching her walk away through the half-filled tables.

"Yes," said Tyler, reading his son straight through. "I guess you will be." He tacked on no caveats, no conditions. Nor did he intend to lose Carson at the hand of Two Rivers' rough trade. Yuby Wellman didn't know it yet, but he would be Carson's unseen chaperone on the Texas Side tonight.

Shortly after their coffee arrived a man approached the table. He wore a fine brown three-piece broadcloth suit and a beaverskin stetson. His belly stretched the seams of his vest. His cheeks, puffed out, reminded Carson of a brown tree squirrel carrying a load of seeds. A sweeping mustache connected with sideburns that reached his jawline. He smelled of lavender soap and money.

"Mr. Kane!" he said jovially. "It's truly fine to see you again after all this time!"

They shook hands, and Tyler said, "This is my son Carson."

Carson shook a hand that was as soft as a woman's.

"May I join you?" asked the man rhetorically, for he had already commandeered a nearby chair. He settled into it with a sigh, as though standing was too strenuous an activity for him.

"This is Ernest Sigel," Tyler informed Carson. "He's a cattle buyer."

"And a square dealer, as well," laughed Sigel heartily.

"As long as you don't give him any other choice," rejoined Tyler, and Carson wasn't sure whether his father was joking or not.

Sigel mustered a hurt expression. "Why, Tyler! Have I ever done wrong by you?"

Tyler gave his almost-smile. "You did right by me two years ago. You gave me fourteen dollars a head, signed, sealed and delivered."

The buyer looked suddenly crestfallen. He was, Carson sensed, a man of many moods, none of them genuine. Sigel shook his head, and Carson half-expected tears to well up into his fugitive eyes.

"The market is not very strong this year, I'm sorry to say. Top price will be ten dollars, I judge. Of course, as we have prearranged, that would come to eight dollars per for you, Tyler."

Carson was stunned and looked at his father, expecting an explosion. But Tyler sat very still, his face an expressionless mask.

"What happened, Ernest?" he asked quietly.

Sigel shrugged. "That's the way with commodities, Tyler. When you brought your first herd up to Sedalia twelve or so years ago you had precious little competition. The war was not long over. The East was starved for beefsteak. But every year more and more ranchers moved their stock to the railhead. It's supply and demand, you see. I'm afraid the factors are balancing out."

Tyler looked out the window, but he didn't see the street. It was the future he was contemplating, and he didn't much care for what he saw.

"I'll be damned."

Sigel went on to add insult to injury. "The cattle business has been so lucrative that foreign investors and Eastern combines have bought into the act. We are talking big money here, Tyler. These men have pooled their resources to buy ranches up north in Montana and Wyoming mostly. A lot of them never take an active part in it. They hire professionals and pay top dollar. They can afford to. It's not make-or-break in their case, the way it is for you Texas cattlemen. It's almost a sideline for them. They just stand under the vine and let the grapes fall. And worst of all, from your perspective, is that they are breeding shorthorns, and the shorthorn makes for a more tender cut than your stringy, tough-as-saddle-leather longhorns."

Carson struggled within himself to sort out a jumble of emotions. He had seen his father work himself and his men from dawn till dusk ever since he could remember. Tyler Kane had carved his own personal empire out of the wild West Texas plains, and it had required a lot of blood and sweat and fierce determination. It had cost them all dearly. And now this well-fed, smooth-talking money man was telling them that it hadn't been worth all the trouble. They had busted their butts for nothing.

Sigel, Carson also noted, spoke of the inevitable catastrophe with the easy objectivity of one who was not a victim but merely an interested observer. This rankled Carson, so he said, "Mr. Sigel, if that's where the money is, why are you here?"

Sigel looked at Carson and then quickly back to Tyler, as though startled by the query. His glance at Tyler held an inquiry of its own.

"I haven't told him," said Tyler, talking to Sigel but watching his son closely. "But I reckon it's his due." He made a small, casual gesture that the cattle buyer took as a go-ahead.

"Carson, you make a good point," smiled Sigel. "Under ordinary circumstances, in fact, I wouldn't be here. I have investors to answer to myself, and to be perfectly honest I would not even pay ten dollars per for a Texas herd this year. It's too chancy. However, in exchange for a favor, your father has agreed to sell me his cows for twenty percent less than the top price. It was an agreement we made almost two years ago. My investors can still realize a profit if I buy at eight dollars. Of course, this will be the only Texas herd I'll purchase this season, for I doubt any of Tyler's colleagues would make their mark on a similar deal."

"I'm not stupid," barked Carson angrily. "I know what the favor was. You're the one who sent that telegram, weren't you, Mr. Sigel? And that's why that hardcase Reese rides with us."

"Who is Reese?" Sigel asked Tyler, but Kane ignored him. Slumped back in his chair, his gaze was fixed on Carson beneath brooding brows.

"I don't think I care for your tone of voice, boy," he said.

"And I don't care for what you're doing," shouted Carson, his heart pounding in his chest. He had never stood up this hard against his father before, and he was scared to death and oddly elated at the same time. "You are selling us all short just to have your revenge. All of us—the boys, Yuby, Banjo, me. And yourself. Worst of all, you hire some dirty gunslinger to do your work for you. I didn't think you were scared of anything. Guess I was dead wrong."

A muscle twitched in Tyler's jaw. His hands, resting on the table, bunched up into white-knuckled fists. Sigel looked like a rabbit ready to run, for he realized that the boy had in effect called Tyler Kane a coward, and he had been around these prideful Texans long enough to expect violence to attend such loose talk.

But Tyler didn't explode, much to the amazement of the others. His wrath melted into sadness, a soft rain on his damaged heart. The walls of anger crumbled and the light of reason struck him like a fence post laid across his forehead. Carson was right all the way. The boy's resentment was fully justified. Problem was, Kane sensed that he was too far down the road to turn around.

"Keep your voice down, son," he said mildly, and looked at Sigel. "Only one thing I want to know. Is Stanhouse here?"

Sigel nodded. His ebullience was gone. Carson's outburst had worked on him, too, bringing the truth home brutally. He could call it business, but facts were facts, and he envisioned himself sitting here now as a conspirator in a scheme to commit murder. The revelation of Reese was like a dose of cold water to his private parts. It broke his spirit, soured the deal. His voice got lackluster.

"He's here. Works a table at Clyde Hobart's place, The Palace. He came back down in early summer, out of the goldfields. Hobart took him in. I hired a Pinkerton man to track him down, for at the time I was in St. Louis. When I heard, I came out for my own look, then wired you." He didn't say, as he might have in other circumstances, that the detective had cost him a pretty penny. His profits off the Triangle transaction would cover that ten times over, for he intended to pocket the twenty percent, representing the actual purchase price to those for whom he fronted as ten dollars per, rather than eight.

"Fair enough," said Tyler soberly. "The inspectors are probably out with the herd now. We'll sign the papers after breakfast. And then we'll go to the bank. I need to pay my hands their wages, for tonight they'll want to go to town."

Carson stood up. "I've lost my appetite. Think I'll ride back to camp." He looked at Sigel with hostility, and at Sigel's belly. "Looks like you know how to eat. Help yourself to my vittles, if they ever get here." And he turned to walk away, his spurs singing on the floor.

Watching him go, Tyler had the feeling that he had lost both his sons, not just the one.

Chapter Nine

Brackett delivered the fine collected on the RD Connected boys to Leon McKaskle and proceeded on down Main to Argie's barbershop. Neither the shebang or the barber shop were very far from the jail, but it was his habit to always have the thoroughbred at close reach. He could get from one side of Two Rivers to the other in a New York minute that way. Contrary to what some others thought, it wasn't conceit that kept him on horseback as he roamed the town. Just a trick of the trade.

He entered Argie's to find a man occupying the barber chair, his body covered by a white sheet, his face wrapped in a hot moist towel. Argie was rinsing his straight razor in a metal basin as he looked around to identify the marshal.

"Just finishing up with this gentleman, Clem. Be right with you."

With a nod Brackett sat on a bench near the window. The shop was a short and narrow room, warmed toastily by a White Oak stove in back, and heavy with the redolence of after-shave fragrances. Argie began to sharpen the razor on a leather strop. He was a short, roly-poly man with a few strands of black hair plastered to his balding scalp with pomade. He had been severely shortchanged in the height department; he used a sturdy wooden produce box beside the barber chair to elevate himself when working.

"How is Mrs. Brackett?" asked Argie amiably.

"Fine."

"Doc Milby was in earlier. Said he was going to drop in on her this morning and see how she is coming along."

"Damn," breathed Brackett, "I forgot about that." The sawbones had alerted him last week that Maris had been included in his Thursday rounds, and would be so until the birth. Brackett concluded that there was no way out of his obligation to be there when the doctor called. He checked the stubble on his cheeks and judged that he would have time for a shave. The least he could do would be to look halfway respectable. And the routine of relaxing under Argie's expert hand and listening to the barber's town gossip had become a pleasant ritual, one he was loathe to forsake.

Argie turned the chair on its swivel so that the man sitting in it could see himself in the wall mirror the moment the towel was removed. Brackett was idly aware of the way the man turned his head this way and that, checking both sides of Argie's handiwork, as the barber laid the cooling towel aside and rubbed a dash of French Quinine on his hands. Then Brackett shifted slightly on the slats of the bench, and the slanting morning sun ricocheted off the polished star pinned to his shirt. The man in the chair didn't move his body one iota, but his gaze, by way of the mirror, locked onto the badge with such intensity that Brackett felt the scrutiny before he even saw it. The man allowed Argie to apply the smell-pretty but acted impatient during the ministration, and at the end he threw the shroud aside before Argie could remove it with his customary flourish. He came out of the chair, long and lean, unwinding with the slick motion of a snake, and Brackett noted the long gray duster and the buckskin leggins only briefly, instinctively focusing on the matching pair of Smith & Wesson .44's at the man's sides.

Reese turned quickly to square off. That, Brackett realized, was pure habit in a man so long wary of the law that it was second nature to expect a problem from a starpacker. Clem

80

kept his posture relaxed. Reese pursed his lips, slowly raised his hands, and ran them through his lank black hair, pulling it out of his face. Then he smiled.

"Howdy."

Brackett gave that a nod. In a flash of intuition he knew that this was the man Eli Kesserling had mentioned earlier. The one with the fancy saddle. Hard on the heels of intuition came the voice of experience. This kind brought trouble with them wherever they wandered, sure as cockleburs on a coyote. Brackett watched him thoroughly as he paid Argie and moved to collect his hat from the brass wall rack—a gray, broad-brimmed hat embellished with a rattlesnake skin band.

"Haven't seen you in Two Rivers before," Brackett remarked.

"First time, and just arrived." Reese started for the door.

"Passing through or here on business?"

That stopped Reese. With a lazy smile of mild reproof he gave Brackett a sidelong glance.

"I'll be moving along before you know it."

Brackett felt like he had to know what this gunslinger was made of. It was generally a case of bad manners to pry into a stranger's affairs, but the badge and the job cut him some slack in that respect. So he stood up, neither too quick nor too slow in his movements, and watched Reese steel himself.

"If you happen onto the Texas Side tonight, be sure to check those pistols. Just the way you wear them is an invitation."

"To what?"

"For a crazy-drunk drover to play the fool."

"I'll remember you said that," replied Reese, and went on out.

Flapping the cover, Argie said, "I'm ready for you, Clem."

Brackett took the chair. "Keep me turned facing the door."

"Don't go making me edgy," admonished Argie, brandishing the straight razor.

* * *

Freshly shaved, Brackett skipped breakfast and rode back out the Kearney road to the house. The day was warming up. South of town, dust from the stockyards and the herds beyond bleached the blue out of the sky.

Doc Milby had already arrived. Horse and buggy stood off the road in the speckled shade of a sycamore. A barefoot boy sat on the weather-warped steps of the porch, whittling on a stick with a Barlow clasp knife. He looked up at the sound of Brackett's approach, and his round, freckled face lit up with a radiant smile as he identified the marshal. Too excited to sit, he jumped to his feet and waited for Brackett to dismount. Clem draped his reins over the porch rail. The boy was ten-year-old Davey Lake, the son of a tanner and his wife who lived in the house to the east. They had come to town last summer, and Davey had immediately latched onto Brackett with an idol worship that fashioned the lawman into the living image of the wild frontier's bigger-than-life hero. Davey's starry-eyed adulation made Brackett uncomfortable even as it flattered him.

"How long has Doc been here?" he asked, watching the house uncertainly, wondering whether it was best to barge in or wait for the word out here.

"I dunno," said Davey, gazing at the star on Brackett's shirt with private rapture. "Not very long."

"Why aren't you in school, boy?" Brackett demanded, holding back the smile that tried to come each time he saw the way the youngster looked at him.

Davey screwed up his face. "I don't like school. What good is all that? I need to learn how to shoot and how to ride."

"You reckon?"

"Yessir, I reckon."

Brackett eased down onto the steps. Davey sat alongside. Now he was ogling the Remington on Brackett's hip, so close that it made his fingers itch just to touch it. Brackett took his time rolling a smoke. When he had the quirling lit he took a drag and then let go a few smoke rings. Davey watched this and was amazed. Everything Brackett did awed him.

"What's that inside your shirt, Davey?" asked Clem, looking off into the yonder.

Davey grinned, brushing untamed, wheat-colored hair out of his face.

"Nobody can put one over on you, can they, Marshal Brackett?" He took the dog-eared penny dreadful out from under his calico shirt and offered it to Brackett, who examined it with some curiosity.

"The Ringo Kid, hmm? Pretty fancy colors. Why, that almost looks like a horse. Is that a horse, Davey? Or an overgrown armadillo?"

Davey broke into that infectious honking laugh of his, and Brackett couldn't resist grinning now.

"I bet they write a book like that about you someday, Marshal Brackett."

"You think so?"

"Sure they will. Why wouldn't they?"

"Oh, I don't know."

"Well, they will, because you're a real, honest-to-God hero, for one thing." Davey said it as though it was as indisputable as sunrise.

"What's a hero, anyway?"

Davey's brow wrinkled. "Well, I guess it's a man who ain't afraid of nothing."

"No, that sounds like a fool or a dead man to me."

"Have you ever been afraid?"

"Many times. Seems like I'm always afraid of something or other." Brackett's thoughts turned to Maris and the baby, and he had the impression that his life was being swept away in the current of change and that he was powerless in its grip.

Perplexed, Davey sobered as he watched the worry in his idol's sun-darkened face. He stood fast in his conviction that Clem Brackett was a genuine hero. It would take more than Brackett's denial to change his mind on that score. On the other hand, every word the marshal uttered the boy took as gospel. So Davey had to reconcile himself to the fact that heroes could be afraid.

"Well," he said finally, drawing out the word, seeing things with the simple logic of a young and uncluttered mind, "I guess a hero is a man who does what he has to do even when he's afraid to do it."

It was Brackett's turn to be amazed. "Maybe you're right, Davey. And I reckon that man would see something through even though he hated it with a passion."

But Davey was as crafty as an old maverick steer that dodged into brush seeing a cowboy's loop coming down.

"I'm too young to be a hero. And I don't like school. I don't like sitting on a hard bench indoors all day long. It makes my butt hurt, for one thing. And I don't like Miss Pierce. She is always rapping my knuckles with her pointin' stick."

"Miss Pierce," smiled Brackett, "is life."

He heard the door open behind him, and stood up as Doc Milby emerged into the cold shade of the dogtrot. Milby was a cadaverous man, unusually tall. He walked slightly hunched over, as though embarrassed by his height, and he always had a sour look on his face, like a man too-long acquainted with pain and misery. It struck Brackett that God had given some of Argie's height to Milby, and all of Milby's good spirits to the barber. Even though Brackett had never know Milby to look any other way but morose, he was nonetheless alarmed.

"Is everything all right, Doc?" he asked, rising quickly. "Is Maris okay?"

Milby spared Brackett the merest glance as he went down the steps between Clem and the boy, his black leather grip in one hand, the other fishing a stemwinder out of his vest watch pocket.

"There's nothing wrong with her. Physically."

Brackett heard the implication and turned defensive. "Are you trying to tell me something?"

In the dust of the yard Milby stopped and half-turned.

"She needs plenty of rest. What she doesn't need is worry.

When she is with child is when a woman most needs her man's compassion and understanding. And when a man becomes a father he has to think about his wife and his child as well as himself, all in equal measures. Becoming a father is a gift from God, Mr. Brackett. Every privilege has its price." Milby sighed. "When I came out of the Ohio Medical Institute I was foolish enough to believe that I could heal the body with the tools of my profession and the skills I had learned. But I found out the hard way that you must first heal the soul. If the mind is ailing or the heart is breaking then nothing I have in this grip will work as it should."

Brackett nodded. "All right, Doc. I get the message."

"It would be tragic if you weren't around to hold your baby in your arms, sir. Believe me, there is no greater moment in a man's life. Equally tragic is a boy growing up without the guidance of a loving father." Milby looked at Davey, standing in Brackett's shadow. "That is a man's most lasting accomplishment. But I think you know what you should do without a sermon from an old sawbones. I'll be back around next Thursday. If you need me before then you know where to find me. Good day."

Watching Milby climb into the buggy and take the reins from around the stock, Brackett heard that door behind him again, and turned to Maris as she came out into the dogtrot, pulling a pale blue wrapper tightly about her. He went to her with eager strides, drawn to her like a moth to flame. She melted into his embrace and rested her head against his shoulder. Brackett smelled the fragrance of her golden hair, the scent of a spring day in the mountains, and felt the firm bulge of their baby between them. And he felt complete.

"I'm sorry about last night, Clem," she said, her voice small and muffled by his coat.

"You shouldn't be."

"But I knew what you were when I married you. Wearing a star has always been your pride. It's part of the man I love."

"It's just a job. I've got something better than a star now.

I'm going to give it up, Maris. I don't need it anymore."

She pulled away slightly to search his eyes, seeing there conviction devoid of doubt.

"Clem, you don't have to . . ."

He put a finger to her lips. "I have a bigger and better job ahead of me. There is a parcel of land down the Platte about twenty miles . . ."

"Clem!" she cried in disbelief.

He grinned. "What? You don't think I haven't given it some thought? There are willows by the river, and elm and maple on a hillside that begs for a house. It is thick with grama. An ohlinger-here place if ever there was one. I'm no farmer but I know a thing or two about horses. And Fort McPherson will be a day's ride away. The army is forever on the lookout for remounts. That animal you see over there is blooded stock. I reckon he'll do, and then some, to start up with."

Her hazel eyes burned with a special light. "And I'll be the luckiest, happiest, proudest woman in Nebraska."

"Then it will be worth it."

Their lips met, a long and lingering kiss full of passion and promise, and Brackett thought he felt the invisible ropes that bound him so mercilessly to the dark and violent side of Two Rivers—the ropes that this woman's abiding love had frayed—unravel completely now and come apart.

Heels rapped imperiously on the porch planking and they separated and turned, still touching, to confront Miss Pierce, the schoolmarm. Miss Pierce had iron-gray hair pulled back in a severe bun, a somber brown serge dress, and heavy brogans. Hands planted on ponderous hips, Miss Pierce glowered at them with stern disapproval. Davey, of course, had made for tall timber.

"Marshal," she barked, "have you seen David Lake?"

"No, ma'am," lied Brackett. With a small shock he realized that the boy's penny dreadful was still in his hand. But the schoolmarm did not seem to notice. She bestowed a frosty once-over upon him.

"If you do, you bring him to me. Truancy is a social crime."

"Yes, ma'am. I'll track him down and bring him to justice."

"It is not a matter to be taken lightly," she scolded. "The boy must learn discipline. It is my duty to at least acquaint the little savage with civilized behavior, to expose him to a few of the most basic social graces. Such as, for instance, what to do, and what *not* to do, in public. If you get my meaning."

Brackett was too happy with the world to do anything but grin like a fool at the sharp-tongued spinster.

"Miss Pierce," he said, with a sincerity she found suspect, "if we had more people like you, and less like me, we'd have this wild country tamed in no time."

"That," declared the schoolmarm, on her way back out to the road, "is manifestly true."

Chapter Ten

Lee Stanhouse stood at the window of his second-floor room in The Plainsman, watching the sun decline in sweeping flourishes of purple and rose beyond the rooftops of Two Rivers. The natural beauty of sunset did not register with him. His hooded, world-weary eyes saw it only as a signal. Another night approaching. The drovers would begin to pour in from the herd camps. Fresh victims. Stanhouse felt a new vitality sweep through him. Gambling was more than a living in his case. It was the breath of life itself. It was so because he gambled more than money. It was his own doing, the way he wanted it, that his very life turned on each card. He played against the sharp eye and the swift-rising temper and the fast gun of the Texas cowboys who sat at his table in The Palace. He felt most alive when he played with death.

And when, he mused, *even that fails finally to move me, I will let myself grow careless.* In that way he controlled his own destiny, free to choose the time and place he departed this veil of tears.

Stanhouse turned into the well-appointed room. He lived comfortably on the wages of sin, even after Hobart skimmed his take off the top of the money he purloined from the cowboys. Going to the dresser, he rinsed his hands with fresh water in a porcelain basin, dried them, and then applied a lotion made from cream and aloe and oat flour. He kept his hands soft so that he could feel the trim and mark of his decks.

The room was darkening. Stanhouse did not care for shadows. He lit a milk-glass lamp standing on the night table. Then he moved to a small parfleche trunk over on the chest at the foot of the bed. Lifting the lid, he gazed fondly at the tools of his trade. The top basket contained thirteen decks of cards. All but a few of them were marked decks, manufactured to his specifications by the New York firm of E. N. Grandine. Some of the crooked decks were "reader" cards with subtle secret markings on their backs. Most, though, were "strippers," their edges trimmed in certain ways.

When he employed a marked deck, Stanhouse preferred to play both ends against the middle, using strippers. Now he took one of these decks, sat down in a high-backed chair of red velvet upholstery and rich hand-carved walnut. He began to limber his fingers—fingers that were a blur of confident motion as he practiced what he already had down to perfection, the false shuffle and the false cut. Alice Ivers had once proclaimed his to be the best hands in the business, the supreme compliment from the high priestess of the game. But still he practiced, daily and without fail. A man could not be too proficient when his livelihood—and his life—depended entirely upon his expertise.

He was dealing seconds onto the side table when a knock came on the door. Stanhouse knew it was Clyde Hobart. The saloon owner had decided on his own accord that he would signal with two quick taps, followed after a pause by one more, when arriving at the gambler's door. It was a precaution that Stanhouse believed unnecessary and found amusing. From the moment he had discovered the gambler's propensity for cheating, Clyde had just assumed that Stanhouse kept his door bolted and his derringer in hand for fear that someday his sins would catch up with him. The truth was, Stanhouse never locked his door and he never looked over his shoulder.

He got up and let Hobart in.

"Ready for another big night, Lee?"

"I'm always ready," replied Stanhouse. No matter who he addressed, or what he said, his tone was always soft and sardonic. "Come to walk me over?"

"No hurry. Just came by to see how you were. Had supper down in the dining room." Hobart watched the gambler intently, as one would watch a person recently recovered from a serious illness but still subject to relapse. "Have you eaten?"

"I lost my appetite years ago."

Hobart frowned and turned away so that Stanhouse wouldn't see it. He had long since given up on inviting the gambler to dine with him. Always so frustratingly polite and proper, Stanhouse had deflected every friendly overture. Nowadays Hobart permitted others, including Stanhouse, to think that he continued to be solicitous only because the gambler made tremendous profits for The Palace. Hobart tried to believe it himself, because he couldn't honestly fathom his very real concern for the well-being of Lee Stanhouse.

"You know," said Hobart, with a gentle reprimand, "one day the wrong fella is going to look into your box of tricks here. Next thing you know you'll feel the rough tickle of hemp around your throat."

Stanhouse closed the door. Hobart lifted up the top basket and looked with troubled brow at the sleeve and breastplate holdout rigs, the "bugs," the card pricker, and the ivory-handled trimmer. Stanhouse went back to his chair.

He said, "This morning I dreamed that there was a knock at my door. An inexplicable, paralyzing fear overcame me. A certainty that something horrible had just come calling. But I was driven to answer. With every faltering step I screamed silently at myself to turn away. But I couldn't turn away. It was a pull that I simply couldn't resist. And I opened the door with a cry of sheer terror on my lips."

An unpleasant tingle rose up his spine as Hobart stared at the back of the gambler's well-groomed head. "Who was at the door, Lee?" he asked finally.

"Death," said Stanhouse, quite nonchalant. "In a cloak that reeked with the foul stench of Hell. Black, eternal emptiness beneath the hood. A fleshless hand reaching out for me."

"One helluva dream," muttered Hobart uneasily.

"I've had it before. Several times. More frequently of late."

Hobart didn't know how to respond. He watched Stanhouse deal a hand onto the sidetable from the bottom of the deck. That was only a hunch, for he couldn't actually *see* the bottom deal, no matter how closely he looked. Stanhouse possessed a talent that never ceased to amaze him. He was the best that Hobart had seen, and Hobart had seen many a cardsharp come and go.

"I can't figure you out, Lee," he confessed. "I just don't savvy why you run a brace when you have the wherewithal to beat others with honest skill. You don't need all this deadweight."

"Of course I don't." Stanhouse sounded surprised that Hobart hadn't yet put his finger on it.

"Then why?"

"Any sensible, cool-headed man with a good memory and decent instincts could beat those yokels in a straight game. But not one in ten thousand can bottom deal with three maddrunk, gun-happy cowboys watching his every move like vultures. Not and get away with it, anyway."

Hobart drew a long breath. "So it's the risk you're after."

"You could say that."

"I hate to see it. You're going to play out your string, Lee. You'll go to an early grave."

"I appreciate your concern. I know it has nothing to do with the fact that you take two bits out of every dollar I make, just for watching my back."

Hobart was stung, and he faltered in his resolve to keep things on the level of business. He didn't know how to express his friendship, especially to a man who acted like he didn't want or need friends.

"It could be you wrong me there," he answered stiffly. "You

may be a cheat, but at least you're a gentleman about it."

Stanhouse laughed softly. "Thank you, Clyde. That's a splendid endorsement. Put it on my headstone, won't you?" Slipping the deck into the side pocket of his black frock coat, he went to the dresser. Fastening the neck of his white, frill-fronted shirt, he found a black string tie in one of the drawers and put it on. He saw Hobart's frown in the oval mirror above the dresser and suddenly felt charitable. Leaving the impudence out of his voice, he said, "Don't read me wrong. I am grateful for your sponsorship. You don't care to show it that often, but you have a big heart when it comes to strays like me. But you would give yourself some quarter if you didn't try to strike up a friendship with people you know nothing about."

"That's just it. I like to understand the people who work my tables. I've known you for the better part of three years, Lee, and yet I know nothing at all about you."

"It's a sorry tale of woe," replied Stanhouse, with only a trace of bitterness. "There is no hell worse than the one a man makes for himself."

He gathered up two more crooked decks, closed the trunk and then, taking pity on Hobart, put a hand on the saloon owner's shoulder.

"Don't worry yourself, Clyde. I'm not ready to cash in, not right yet."

"We don't always have a say as to when that happens."

"Oh, but we do," corrected Stanhouse glibly. "We always have a say."

He went on by, opened the door, and with a courtly, refined gesture, let Hobart precede him out into the hall.

"I feel lucky tonight," he exclaimed, feeling new life run streaming through his veins.

Chapter Eleven

"Want another one?" asked Magruder as he pushed himself across the book-lined study to the sideboard to refill the empty shot-glass in its armrest hole. It was a rhetorical question, a polite gesture, for Ernest Sigel, the cattle broker, had not touched a drop of his own. He sat looking miserable and confused in the red leather wing chair over by the window, the spot Clem Brackett always sought when he came by. Sigel was leaning forward as much as the bulk of his belly would permit. He looked like a man getting hit with the first symptoms of what was bound to be a long and wracking illness. The shot-glass was held in both hands before him, his elbows resting on his knees. The bottom of the glass rested in the palm of his left hand, and the beefy fingers of his right encircled the rim, turning the glass slowly, first one way and then the other.

The question surprised Sigel and brought him momentarily back into the room, for he had been staring at the floor in front of him, a prisoner of morose contemplation. He had forgotten about his drink. Now he looked at it, understood the query, and shook his head. Turning his head, he gazed out the window, and saw the half-light of dusk filling Yellowtooth with its indistinct grayness. Magruder already had a couple of Rochester lamps burning, and the room was warm and gold.

"This is a good room," remarked Sigel. "Makes me think for a moment that I am back in a civilized place. Not some wide-open trail town. This is a room that belongs in St. Louis, not Two Rivers."

Magruder was coming back, his glass once again filled to the rim with the hot amber of Overholt. Stopping directly in front of Sigel, Magruder lifted the glass in a toast.

"Here's to long ropes and loose hobbles," he intoned, and took a long sip.

Sigel gave him a crooked smile. "I don't know about you, Mac. You're a man of two different worlds."

"Who belongs to neither," added Magruder cheerfully.

"Well, I don't belong out here, that's plain to see. I don't understand these Westerners and their frontier mentality. I thought I did but I was only fooling myself." He shook his head.

"One question, Ernest. Why did you bring this to me?"

"Isn't that obvious? Everybody knows you and Marshal Brackett are good friends. I can't go straight up to the marshal."

"Why not?"

Sigel's demeanor reflected self-contempt. "Because I'm afraid of Tyler Kane."

"He didn't tell you to keep it a secret. It's not like you're breaking your bond."

"No, he didn't. He didn't have to. He doesn't expect me to be bothered with ethical considerations. But I feel like I am double-dealing all the same. I will make a lot of money on the transaction for the Triangle herd. That was the price for my cooperation. Now that the contract is signed and the money exchanged I am running off to blow the whistle. Now it's done.

My conscience should be feeling better. I wonder why it isn't, Mac?"

"In every aspect of life except business, Ernest, you are an impeccably decent man."

Sigel looked like he had been slapped across his puffy jowls. "You just come right out and say what you think, don't you?"

"Am I wrong? I'm not condemning you. You have a job to do and you do it extremely well. You believe that men should play by the rules in society. And you believe there are no rules in business. That's the mark of a civilized man. But men so utterly civilized don't quite fit in out here. Not yet. Soon enough, but not yet."

"What Kane is planning amounts to cold-blooded murder. I don't care what kind of society this is, I don't think you could call it anything else. And I can't just stand by and do nothing about it."

"You've done something. You came to me."

"And what will you do?"

Magruder took another shot of bourbon, licked his lips, and looked at his emaciated legs beneath the red and black blanket. His demeanor was moody and distant.

"You don't need to worry yourself about it from here on," he assured the cattle broker. "What I'm telling you is that your conscience ought to be clear. It's not now only because you won't let it be. Walk away from this and don't look back. You have handed me the problem. That was the right thing to do, because you can't handle it and I can."

Sigel sighed. "Lord, I wish it were that easy. Thing is, I knew from the first that I was buying into something that was . . . that was morally corrupt. I knew when Kane sent me that first letter, offering me the deal if I could locate this Stanhouse fellow, that he wanted the gambler for a reason. And it wasn't just to give him a good talking-to. It was vengeance. I am the Judas Iscariot in this little drama, Mac. I've got the thirty pieces of silver to prove it."

"You're not standing in the right place to look at it and see it for what it really is," commented Magruder. "The New Testament has not yet come out this far west. What Kane has in mind is not peculiar at all. He is a Westerner. He is doing what he has to, or he'll never know peace in his own soul. We live by a somewhat different code of conduct in these parts, Ernest, than they do in St. Louis. You may think you understand men like Tyler Kane because you have cut a half-hundred deals with them. But that was business. And there are no rules in business. This is life. Out here we have certain rules. A quick and easy way of seeing law and order maintained. No frills and no fancy words. Every man must see to his own protection. If he is unable or unwilling to take some responsibility for his own welfare then he had better get the hell back east of the Big Muddy. He cannot count on the law or its representatives to do the job for him. If two men have differences, they are expected to settle those differences between themselves. If it's a fair fight, that's okay. If it isn't a fair fight, the law must step in and balance the scales. And if the law can't, or won't, then mob rule takes over. Everyone who survives out here accepts that code. There is a common consent. It is sometimes cold-hearted and brutal, but when you think about it you can discover its merits."

"But Kane has bought himself a hired killer," protested Sigel. "That's what Kane's boy said. Is that in keeping with your code of justice, Mac? I might have walked away from this, kept my big mouth shut, except for that revelation."

Magruder frowned. "In that respect it would seem that Tyler Kane has stepped over the line. Generally you hire a gun only if you need it to even the odds."

"Maybe Kane is getting too civilized," said Sigel caustically. "He bought me and this fellow Reese to do his dirty work for him."

Magruder looked at Sigel with pity. The cattle buyer fully intended to carry a cross. It was self-inflicted punishment, the price Sigel had decided he should have to pay. No one could lift that burden from his shoulders but Sigel himself, and only when in his own mind he could conclude that he had suffered enough for his sins.

"Maybe he thinks he *is* evening the odds," offered Magruder thoughtfully. "You know these Texans think that almost everybody in a trail town—the marshal, the merchants, the saloon owners, the gamblers, and the girls, all of them—conspire to relieve the drover of his pay."

Sigel sighed again and knocked back the bourbon, gasping as it flamed down his pipes. Then he put the glass on a table and stood up, tugging at his vest and sleeves to get his fine hand-tailored clothes into place. He could not pull all his dignity back into place, though.

"I'll be going, Mac," he said. "Thanks for the drink." He came forward and put out his hand, gratefully surprised that Magruder reached up and shook it firmly. "I won't be back this way again. I have bought my last Texas longhorn."

Magruder nodded. "*Adios,* Ernest. Leave the door open, will you?"

Sigel collected his beaverskin stetson and left the room.

A moment later Daybreak appeared in the doorway. She saw her father sitting in a pool of golden light from one of the lamps, his chin resting on his chest.

"Father," she said, alarmed, going to him. "Are you ill?"

"Sick in my heart, child," he replied.

She sank to her knees beside the wheelchair and laid her hand on his arm.

"You must warn him."

"It will drag him back into the thick of things." Disconsolate, he stroked her gleaming black hair. "The best thing for Clem Brackett would be to take off his star and pack himself and Maris right out of here."

She stood up sharply and backed up a few steps, out of his reach. "No. How can you say that, Father?"

The anguish in her eyes and in her voice was his anguish, too. "Dammit, girl! Don't you think I know how you feel about him? A blind man could see it."

"You think *she* is right for him and that I am not."

"That's a helluva thing to say."

"It is a true thing to say," she snapped. "You are ashamed that you took my mother as your woman. You do not want your friend to suffer as you have, to be cast out by his own people as a squaw man."

"You cut like a knife with words like those," he muttered, hoarse with strong emotion.

"You say she is good for him. I say she is not. She tried to change him into a different man. I love him for what he is. She is selfish and thinks only of her own needs. She gives no thought to his."

"And you do? You want to go tell him what Sigel told me? Then go ahead. And if he gets killed trying to stop Kane and his gunslinger, what will you say then?"

She was silent for a moment, giving the question serious consideration, and Magruder entertained a fleeting hope that his argument had changed her mind. But the hope was forlorn. Daybreak lifted her chin, and he saw the defiance blazing in her dusky eyes.

"Then I will say he died like a man, not running away."

Magruder suddenly lost the will to fight. He rolled himself over to the sideboard. He reached for the decanter, for the only solace left to him. Daybreak had never challenged him like this. Now he realized that it was not entirely unexpected. Her accusation concerning his motive for trying to keep her and Brackett apart was, perhaps, closer to the mark than he cared to believe. He didn't know. He couldn't be sure. He was confused, and self-doubt defeated him.

"Go on, then," he muttered. "I can't stop you. I wouldn't even try. Maybe I'm wrong. God knows, I hope that I am. But the way I see it, and any way it goes, child, you are in for a broken heart."

There was no reply, and when he glanced back into the room he found her gone.

Chapter Twelve

Tyler Kane found Banjo Stubbins rattling around his Studebaker chuckwagon. The cook had staked out a tarpaulin on poles and had attached it to the end of the wagon. Shelter was a luxury for Banjo, for during the drive he had been constantly on the move, never in one place long enough to rig such cover. He had a small fire going under the tarp, with a strange-smelling brew bubbling in a kettle hanging from an iron pot rack. A stone's throw away, over a sandy cutbank under some dusty cottonwoods, a bigger fire blazed and crackled, dispelling the chill of nightfall. The Triangle boys—those who had not already lit out for the Texas Side—were whooping it up, were all in a fever trying to dandy up for the occasion.

Kane stepped off his bay and ground-hitched. He had put on a sheepskin coat and rawhide gloves, but the cold had gotten into his joints and he winced as he knelt down by the cookfire beneath the tarp. Banjo had the work table down on its wooden leg and was going through the chuck box, making a list of his needs for the road home. He closed the sourdough keg, licked the end of his stubby pencil, scratched an addition on the piece of paper, and only after that was done did he acknowledge Kane's presence.

"What are you cooking up here?" queried Kane. "Doesn't

smell like any sowbelly and beans I ever got wind of."

Banjo had a peevish look about him. "Didn't you pay the boys off today?"

"I did."

"Ain't they got eateries in Two Rivers?"

"They do."

"Then why in blue blazes should I cook for 'em? Been bustin' my butt to get three squares a day into their faces, without, mind you, even a 'much obliged' for my time and trouble."

"You're a crabby sonuvabitch, Banjo. I just asked you what you had in this kettle."

"Sassafras and ironroot tonic," rasped Stubbins, securing the pencil over his ear. "For when your owlhoots come staggerin' back to camp green to the gills with who-hit-John."

Kane's knees would not abide his hunkered down position, so he stood up, wincing again.

"You got any of that rattlesnake oil left, Banjo?"

Banjo snorted. "What's a young man like you doing with rheumatism? And the answer is no. The cupboard's as bare as a baby's bottom. I got a list of supplies here. You gonna get 'em, or do I?"

"What do you need?"

"What do I need? Oh, not too damned much, Mister Kane. Just flour, coffee, sugar, salt, pintos, vinegar, molasses, matches, bakin' soda, tobacco, needle and thread, calomel, castor oil, a couple bottles of whiskey—for medicinal purposes only, of course—about a hunnerd pounds of taters, oats for my team, axle grease, a spare wheel . . ."

Kane held up his hand. "I haven't got time for that. You go."

"Should I just take it at gunpoint or are you gonna give me a bankroll?"

Kane took a roll of greenbacks from his pocket, peeled off more than a few bills, and gave them to Stubbins. He put the rest back in his pocket. Banjo glowered at him.

"Do I get paid like everybody else or did I just donate all my labor these past three months?"

Kane took the money back out and thinned the roll some more.

"Did we get top dollar for the herd?" asked the cook, mollified.

"Close enough." Kane's voice was terse, and he was quick to change the subject. "Have you seen Carson?"

"Thought he was in town with you."

"Hell," growled Kane.

Reaching under the top half of his under-riggins to scratch at graybacks, Banjo cocked his head to one side and gave Kane a suspicious look.

"You have a fallin' out with that boy, Tyler?"

"Is that any of your business?" barked Kane.

Red in the face, the gristleneck cook yanked the corncob pipe out of the back pocket of his suspendered trousers and chomped down on its tip like a man biting the bullet. Then he stalked off to the tool box over on the right side of the wagon, back under the coffee grinder, and began to rummage around violently.

Kane shook his head and turned to watch the preparations of his punchers. Grady Harmon, with Lon Banks in tow, came galloping by. Grady was flourishing his hat high overhead. "This is our night to howl!" he cried, flushed with a fever pitch of exultation, and then they were gone into the deepening night, quirts snapping.

"Keep your boots on," murmured Kane into their dust.

He heard a rider coming up from the other side and turned to watch Yuby Wellman emerge from the darkness. The foreman dismounted Indian-fashion and moved up under the tarpaulin.

"How's the herd?" asked Kane. They still had to hold the Triangle beeves a couple of days, until room was made for them in the stockyards.

"A mite restless. We're downwind from a lot of strange smells."

"Who's on night guard?"

"Jube and Monte. They won't be singing *"Wrangling Joe"* with much enthusiasm tonight. But they'll stick. And I'll be around."

"No, you won't be. I want you in Two Rivers tonight."

"That's not my style."

"This is a job, not play, that I'm talking about. I want you to find Carson. And once he's found, watch out for him."

The black *segundo's* face was a mask bronzed by the throw of firelight. His brown eyes glimmered like polished tin as they looked right through Kane.

"Carson is a man," he said, finally. "Long past the need for a wet nurse."

Kane put a tight rein on his anger, knowing that it would do no good to come down hard on Wellman.

"If you care what happens to him you'll do as I say. There may be trouble in Little Texas tonight."

Yuby nodded. "I expect. You brought trouble with you."

"I didn't know that was any of your concern."

Wellman tugged thoughtfully on the lobe of his left ear, looked away, and then back.

"You're right. I hope you and everybody else keeps it that way."

"What does that mean, straight out?"

But Wellman turned his back on Kane, mounted his claybank and slipped off into the night.

Maris went all out on supper that night, following up the beef stew and frying pan bread with a wild plum cobbler, Brackett's favorite dessert, a fresh pot of Arbuckle to go with it. She was radiantly happy, and it showed on her lovely face as she sat across the oilcloth-draped table from him in their little kitchen, warmed by the fire in the cannonball stove. He indulged in second helpings and then pushed back, grinning at her.

"I am stuffed to the hairline," he announced.

She rose to gather up the graniteware and he made to assist her, but she pushed him gently back into his chair.

"I'll manage, thank you, sir."

"Doc says you're to take it easy."

"I'm fine. I have never felt so fine."

"Or looked so fine, either. Don't go handing out the rest of that cobbler to Eli Kesserling or the Lakes, now."

"That's not very neighborly," she laughed.

"Well, once I go give McKaskle this badge tomorrow we won't have any money coming in regular. It will take everything we've saved, plus a loan, to buy that parcel. All I'm saying is, we may have to settle for tallow and sorghum as dessert for a spell."

Over at the counter, by the sink and the water pump, Maris grew still, but did not look around. Brackett sensed that he had thrown a shadow over her sunny disposition.

"Second thoughts, Clem?" she asked, trying too hard to keep her tone casual.

"No, ma'am." He rose quickly and went to her, put his arms around her waist and his hands on the miraculous bulge of her belly. "We are going to raise horses for the cavalry and a passel of little Bracketts for Miss Pierce to civilize."

Pressed up against her he felt the stirring of desire in his loins, and his hands began to climb up along her ribcage. Laughing softly, she reached up and arrested them just short of their destination.

"One at a time, Mr. Brackett, if you please," she said, leaning her head back against his shoulder and smiling up at him.

He kissed her hair. "Yes, ma'am. I guess I'd better just amble out onto the porch and have a smoke."

"It's cold out there, Clem," she protested.

"Then I'll cool down in a hurry."

"Put on your coat."

He did so and stepped out into the dogtrot, which was

illumined by a storm lantern hanging on a bent nail. It was full night and the cold struck him sternly, but he barely noticed. His belly was full of warm vittles and his heart with warm feelings. He walked out to the porch and looked across at the town. By now, he mused, the action was picking up in Little Texas. He thought he could hear, very faintly, the rumble of booted feet from the dancehalls, like the sound of a far-off stampede, but he couldn't be sure that it wasn't in his mind. A bone-chilling wind was sweeping down from the north, pressing his clothes against his spine and turning the stretch of buffalo grass before him into a sea of waves touched with the silver of the early moon.

One sound he was certain was not imagination—the clatter of crockery as Maris performed her kitchen cleanup. Taking out his papers and tobacco pouch, he rolled a smoke by touch, and marveled at his feelings. The pull that the Texas Side had once had on him was gone. He searched his soul and could find it lurking nowhere. The agonizing decision had been made. He had been pulled from pillar to post in making it, but now that the deed was done he felt lighthearted and confident of his destiny. He wondered what had made the choice so difficult. Flicking a match to life with his thumbnail, he cupped the flame in his hands and lit the cigarette. He looked up to find Daybreak standing at the foot of the porch steps. The inner warmth of his contentment slipped away and he shuddered as the north wind cut clean through him.

"What's wrong?" he asked grimly.

"There is going to be trouble."

"There's always trouble," he said, almost a lament. "Everywhere we go."

"A man is going to be gunned down."

He saw that, as usual, she was barefoot and wore no wrap over her simple yellow dress, and yet she didn't look as though the cold affected her; in fact, standing there gazing up at him, she looked flushed with a passionate heat. He wanted to curse her but couldn't bring himself to do it.

"Did Mac send you?"

She hesitated, then shook her head. "He did not want you to know."

Brackett nodded. "Figures. We both should have known she wouldn't let me go without a fight."

"She?"

He flung a savage, bitter gesture at the town. "My mistress." He dropped the cigarette and crushed it under his boot. "Wait here."

Entering the kitchen, he found Maris with her back to the counter, waiting for him with an expression that reflected the affliction of dashed hopes. Brackett was sickened by the sight of it.

"Who is that out there, Clem?" she asked, her voice hollow.

"Magruder's daughter." He glanced guiltily at his guns hanging in their rigs on the back of a chair. "Maris . . ."

"Don't say it," she warned him fiercely. "Don't say anything."

"I have to go."

"Do you? You *want* to go. You can't give up the Texas Side. You don't want to be rid of it. You need it as much as Clyde Hobart needs it. I knew I would lose you to it."

"You haven't lost me, Maris."

"Oh, I never had you in the first place!" she cried.

"You said you knew what I was when you married me. Well, I'm still that man. Do you expect me to turn my back on it now?"

"No," she said, and in horror he watched her stumble near the brink of hate. "I don't expect anything from you."

Feeling numb and somehow unreal, Brackett took up his guns. Draping the rig for the Porterhouse over his shoulder, he strapped the Remington's shell belt around his hips. He fumbled with the buckle, feeling punch-drunk, and looked around the little room as though he didn't know quite where he was. The wind, getting vigorous, rattled the panes in the window behind Maris.

"I'll be back."

He watched her and waited, but she said nothing, and the look on her ashen face, as hard and colorless as alabaster, haunted him as he turned away and stepped out into the cold and lonesome night.

Chapter Thirteen

When Tyler Kane rode up to one of the tie rails in front of The Plainsman the north wind was kicking up good. Dust filled the streets with a haze that clogged the nostrils and aggravated the eyes. He had the collar of his sheepskin turned up and the brim of his hat pulled low, and he was hunched in the saddle, for the wind chilled to the bone. He did not need to look up at the sky to know that the stars were falling back before the onslaught of heavy clouds rolling in from the north. Already the quarter moon was wreathed with gossamer wisps. He had seen enough blue northers blow in to know what was coming. There had been a time when Kane had paid the elements no mind. He had been a kind of elemental force himself, with contemptuous disregard for furnace heat and bitter cold. Tonight though, he felt brittle and spent, and he faced the prospect of winter and wondered if he could endure its privations.

Dismounting, he tied rein and stepped up onto the boardwalk. The double doors of the hotel lobby were closed and warm yellow light streamed through the lead-paned glass. The blow had driven most people indoors. He spared the stretch of boardwalk the most cursory of looks, then started inside.

"You looking for me?"

Kane swung around as Reese came up out of a barrel chair and out of the shadow caught between the bars of light from two of the dining room windows. The wind whipped the duster away from his body.

"I thought you'd be inside. What the hell are you doing out here?"

"Getting some air." Reese took a deep breath, and threw his arms out wide in a cat-like stretch, filling his lungs. He acted like he was strolling through a balmy spring day.

"Feels like a storm before sunrise, don't it?" grinned the gunslinger.

"We have to talk."

"Sure we do. We can go on inside if you need to, Mr. Kane."

"No," snapped Kane, annoyed that Reese could tell he was suffering from the weather.

"No, I reckon that wouldn't do, would it? You don't want anyone to know we have business together, do you?"

"We'll talk over here," said Kane curtly.

He turned and went down the Fremont Street leg of the boardwalk, away from the dining room windows. He heard the gunhawk's boots on the planking as Reese followed. Kane would have gone to the end, as far from the lobby doors as he could get, but halfway there he listened to Reese stop and sprawl out on a bench. Kane stopped, too, but he didn't sit down. He kept his back to the pistolman, leaning against an upright over by the railing.

"We don't have any business, Reese," he said. "Not anymore."

Reese didn't answer immediately. Kane wanted very much to turn and face the hired gun, but the motive was fear, so he forced himself to stay the way he was, straining his ears.

"You best speak up, Mr. Kane." Reese's tone had lost that insolently false ring of neighborliness. It had been replaced by something lurid and unsafe. "I might take what you say the wrong way."

"You heard me."

"You get cold feet of a sudden? Is that it?"

"Think what you like," said Kane crossly. "We're through."

"I'm sorely disappointed in you. I took you for a man of your word."

"I never gave you my word on anything."

"I didn't tag along behind your damned herd for three months just to get hog-legged."

"You got paid."

"Yeah. I got paid. But I haven't got to the payoff, yet. We agreed on a tidy little bonus once the job was done. You give me that and maybe I'll go ahead and let you welsh on our deal."

Kane clenched his teeth. What Reese was asking for galled him. But what were the alternatives? Once, maybe, he would have squared off with fire in his eyes and dared to dictate to a mankiller like this one. But now he simply felt old and outmatched.

"You'll have your money in the morning. Ask for it at the desk when you check out."

He thought he heard a soft laugh, but the zephyr was whispering in his ears and the arctic air numbed his face and cut his eyes.

"If that's the way you want it, Mr. Kane." Reese sounded well-disposed again.

"That's the way I want it."

"Just curious. What about the gamblin' man? You make up your mind to go whole-hog and do the deed yourself?"

"I don't know," admitted Kane, a heartfelt answer.

Reese was genuinely interested in what motivated Kane. "I mean, you've been nursing a grudge for a long time. That cardsharp killed your own flesh and blood. It's only fitting that he get what's coming to him. A man don't just up and chuck it all like this, not when he's set his sights on blood vengeance for two years."

"Things change," replied Kane, a bitter irony coming through. "But if any man calls on Lee Stanhouse for payback, it'll be me."

"Thought you wanted to keep your hands clean."

"I thought I had a lot to lose. I was wrong."

Kane didn't bother telling Reese about the way his world had been changed by his talk that morning with Ernest Sigel. About how it looked like the bottom was going to fall out of the Texas cattle trade, and how his personal empire was really only a few hundred square miles of dirt and rock and cactus, good for nothing. And he didn't care to tell the gunslinger that, in his tremendous self-conceit, he had allowed himself to believe that anything he cared to do was acceptable simply because he wanted it done, that it didn't matter what others thought. He still wasn't sure but that the gambler needed to die for shooting down his son. But he had recognized that Tyler Kane was not so high and mighty that he no longer had to play by the rules.

A man came out of the hotel and Kane stiffened. Despite the fact that he had just cut loose from Reese, his association with the gunhawk was still a humiliation—always would be—and he did not care for anyone else to become aware of it. But the man did not even look around; instead, buckling under the blast of the north wind, he pulled up his collar and hurried out of sight around the corner onto the Main Street side.

"There is one other matter," said Kane, eager to be done with Reese. "You rode in here on a Triangle horse. Buy yourself one that hasn't got my brand to ride out on."

There was no response. Kane glanced over his shoulder.

Reese was gone.

Irish Joe Kempen was waiting for the two Triangle punchers when they swung out of Sawdust Sally's, already half-drunk, arms thrown around one another's shoulder, howling a wickedly off-key version of *"My Horse Won't Stand."* They fetched up short and cut out the caterwauling in midverse.

"You lose your hat?" asked Grady Harmon, and Lon Banks giggled. They were saddle partners, but Lon played second

114

fiddle. Grady usually called the shots, and Lon was almost always happy to let him and to follow his lead.

Irish laughed with them in a good-natured way, and that caught Grady off guard, so he started to give Kempen one of his who-the-hell-are-you once-overs. His impertinent survey got no further than the star pinned to Kempen's gunbelt. Irish, standing in a casual, unaggressive, hipshot manner, had his thumbs hooked over his waistband. His stick dangled from his wrist.

"You gentlemen going back to camp this early in the evening?" he asked pleasantly.

"Hell. We just got here."

"I know when you got here. I saw you ride in." Kempen's tone got harder by degrees. "I also see that you forgot to check your guns."

Lon looked down at his shellbelt like he wondered what on earth it was and why it was strapped to his waist. But Grady was on his way to belligerence, and glowered at Irish.

"I was here a couple years ago," he huffed, irritably. "I don't recall any such nonsense."

"A new house rule. Now don't tell me you didn't notice all the other men had lightened their load."

Lon looked at Grady and Grady looked at Irish and Irish looked right back, his green eyes bright and steady and unblinking. They stood like that for a long moment, with the wind howling down the street. Kempen thought, *This one is a hot-blood. His friend will fight like a scrapper, but only if this one starts the dance.* But he didn't push, just waited looking for all the world like he didn't give a hoot which way it went.

Finally Grady said, disgusted, "You mean we have to go back in there and give up our irons before you'll let us walk down the damned street?"

"See how this suits you. Next place you step into, check the guns. Leave 'em there till you're ready to ride out."

His mouth twisted, Grady nodded and said, "Fine."

"Then you won't be bothered by me anymore tonight," said

115

Irish, going around them.

"That breaks my heart," muttered Grady.

But Kempen let him have the last word and walked away, heading north up Smoke toward the deadline. He had already made up his mind to check on the pair during his next round. He wasn't sure that they had got the message.

"Check your guns," sneered Grady once Irish was out of earshot. "Who does he think we are? That's enough to make a cow laugh."

Lon said, "Shoot, Grady. Don't get your hackles up. We're here to have a little fun, right?"

"I'd have some fun lightin' into that pilgrim, I can tell you."

They headed south down Smoke. Grady was chapped because the wind and Irish Kempen had sobered him up. They were about to climb onto the boardwalk fronting The Palace when Grady saw movement in the shadows of the alley to his left. At first he thought it was the starpacker rimwalking them, but it was Carson Kane who stepped out of the trash-littered weeds and into the backlash of light from the front window of the saloon. Grady cooled down.

"Hey, Carson."

"Hello, Grady, Lon."

Grady saw that Carson still wore his sidegun. Lon saw it as well, and it was Lon who said, trying to make it sound like a joke, "They'll make you check your gun, Carson, if you want to stay."

"Will they?" There was a flat and peculiar ring to Carson's voice. "You boys going into The Palace?"

"You bet," said Grady. "Come along with us. There's no better place in Two Rivers to let the he-wolves howl and the panthers prowl."

"Grady," said Carson, his gaze so intense that Grady got uneasy, "you were here two years ago when Murdoch was killed."

Now Grady was cold stone sober. "That's right. I saw it happen. Hell, Carson, I would have plugged that cardsharp on the spot. You know I would have. Except that every dealer and apron in the place filled their hands and got the drop on us."

Carson shook his head. "That doesn't matter now. All I want you to do for me is point out the gambler, Stanhouse. He's supposed to be in there now."

Again Grady looked at Carson's gun. "What do you have in mind?"

"That's not your worry."

"Jesus, Carson," breathed Lon, suddenly *very* worried. "That's what that gunslinger your Pa hired is for, ain't it? Why should we get mixed up in it?"

"Screw down your hull, Lon," snapped Grady. He was afraid, too, but his fear was diluted by a wild and fierce excitement. "How will you do it, Carson? They don't play guns-on-the-table poker in there."

Carson removed the Colt Civilian from its holster, snugged it under his waistband, in the small of his back, under his coat. Then he unbuckled the shellbelt and stashed it beneath the boardwalk's side steps.

"I've already checked my gun," he said.

Grady gave a slow nod, his face flushed with more than the cold. "We're with you, Carson. Ain't we, Lon? I never cottoned to the idea of that Reese fella, anyway. It don't seem right. Us Texans take care of our own business. We've always done."

Carson didn't reply, simply turned and walked, stiff-legged, into The Palace. Grady and Lon followed, the former with enthusiasm, the latter with some reluctance.

A half minute later Yuby Wellman emerged from the alley on the north side of Hobart's saloon. Looking down, he saw the edge of Carson's shellbelt lying under the steps. He nudged it all the way out of sight with the toe of his boot and then strolled on into The Palace.

Chapter Fourteen

"Full house. Jacks over treys."

Stanhouse spread the hand out on the green baize in front of him so that the three drovers at his table could see the cards. He called it without apology and without the loud exultation that most cowboys exhibited when he let them win, because he knew from experience that either attitude could turn a loser bellicose.

"I'll be a son of a gun," groaned the trail hand to his left. "Thought for sure I had you whipped." He threw his cards down on the table, an angry gesture, and Stanhouse studied him closely. But the drover put on a sheepish grin. "I'm busted flat, gents," he confessed to the table with that good-natured acceptance of ill fortune that was one of the best attributes of the Texas cowboy.

The gambler's smile was friendly and compassionate. He had dealt the man three eight-spots and then opened with a modest bid, knowing that the other would take the bait and gamble the rest of his poke. Stanhouse preferred an experienced player on his left, and this one had revealed early on that he had not a lick of poker sense. So Stanhouse had busted him in half an hour.

As the man gathered up to leave, Stanhouse put two silver dollars on the table in front of him. Half out of the chair, the cowboy looked at the money and stopped smiling.

"I don't believe in charity," said Stanhouse. "But I do not permit a man to leave my table flat broke. Ask around if you don't believe that. It's my way. It's bad for business, in my opinion, if I don't do this."

The man looked at the other two drovers at the corner table. One of them shrugged his shoulders, as if to express that he didn't see anything wrong with the gambler's gesture. So the man picked up the coins and gave Stanhouse a nod before heading for the bar.

"Mind if I buy in?"

Stanhouse looked up at Carson Kane as he gathered in the pot from the last game. Carson stood behind the recently vacated chair and Grady Harmon stood behind and to one side of him. The gambler automatically checked to see if they were gunless. That was a house rule as well as a town ordinance. No drover was to participate in a game of chance while carrying. That gave the edge to the house, for all the dealers were armed.

"Be my guest," said Stanhouse, meticulously sorting greenbacks and coin into tidy piles.

Kane sat down without taking his coat off. The gambler made a mental note of that. The Palace was in full swing, jam-packed with men, and while it was winter outside it was comfortable enough in here, with the heat from all the bodies adding to the warmth emanating from iron stoves in the back corners.

Grady was looking around in vain for a chair. "I'll try my luck too," he said.

Polite but firm, Stanhouse said, "Sorry, gent. There's a limit at this table. Too many players slow down the play."

Disappointed, Grady looked at the back of Carson's head. Then he laid a hand on Carson's shoulder and mumbled, "We're with you, *amigo*," and turned to push and shove his way back to the mahogany where Lon Banks waited.

As Stanhouse pulled in the cards and began to shuffle he laid down the rules of his table for the newcomer's benefit.

"There are many variations of the game, sir, but at this table we play draw poker. Dollar ante and no limit on the bet. That may strike you as steep, but the risk sweetens the game. We play table stakes. No man can raise another out of the game. Jacks or better to open. If anyone wants to cut, say so before I begin to deal. If you have to make water, or if you can't wait for one of the girls to make her rounds and take your drink order, than you can leave the table, but I won't hold up the play on your account. Time is money and the night is always too short. If you say so, I'll hold your place, but if you're not back for the third deal you forfeit your chair. Any questions?"

Carson shook his head. He was watching the gambler shuffle the deck. Stanhouse looked like it took as much conscious thought for him to shuffle as it did to breathe. He seemed to pay no attention to what his agile fingers were doing. But after three riffles Stanhouse knew what the first twenty cards were, and what order they were in, for he had rearranged them to his liking. Besides having loaded the bottom of the stripper deck with five more pasteboards of his choice.

"I got a question," said the drover to the gambler's right. He was an older hand with a craggy face and a handlebar mustache gray as iron ore. He sat with his back to the front window of The Palace. Stanhouse had him pegged as an over-cautious player. He did a lot of folding, and if the bets ran too high he would not take a chance on a marginal hand. Lee had dealt him a few winning combinations and had seen how the waddy would bunch up his cards and then fan them out again when he had the makings of a high hand, squinting at them suspiciously, like he couldn't be sure he was reading them right.

"Yes, sir," said Stanhouse.

"What if we want a new deck?"

"Then go to the bar and get one," said the gambler amiably. That didn't bother him. All of Hobart's aprons knew to give out only the decks Stanhouse had brought down and stashed in a particular place under the bar. None of the barkeeps had been told that these were crooked decks. They were accustomed to professionals who were superstitious about the cards they used and were loathe to work a house deck that might be "cold." If they had any suspicions of their own they kept them close to the vest. Lee had learned that aprons as a whole were men who knew how to mind their own business.

"So, gentlemen," said Stanhouse, looking around the table. "Shall we play cards?"

"Deal," said Carson.

A bit earlier Yuby Wellman had stepped into the crowded saloon, spied Carson with Grady and Lon, squeezed in at the bar with their backs to the door, and moved on toward the rear of the long, narrow room. He went to the far end of the mahogany, unbuckled his gunbelt, and handed it over to one of the barkeeps. The backbar consisted of two sections of large pigeonholes; like an oversized mail counter. Each space was numbered. The sections flanked a large, gilt-framed oil painting of a voluptuous, creamy-skinned woman lounging seductively on a burgundy divan, a length of pale yellow material, shiny like satin, draped over her curvy hip and down between her legs.

The apron put Yuby's rig into an available space and gave the Triangle foreman a wooden plaque with the number 31 etched into it. This, Yuby saw, was the number of the pigeonhole now filled with his gun belt. A quick glance told him that there were forty spaces in all, and better than half were now stocked with firearms.

"What's your pleasure?" asked the barkeep, laconic.

Yuby ordered a beer, paid the two bits and took the schooner with him over near the faro table. He leaned against the back wall, where he could get a good view of Carson and the two Triangle hands at the front end of the saloon. Yuby had not been in Two Rivers at the time of Murdoch's death, but he had heard the story time and again in bunkhouse conversation, and he was bright enough to feel certain that the man in black was none other than Lee Stanhouse himself.

Jean Claude, the faro dealer, gave Wellman a speculative

glance as he slipped two cards out of the dealing box, a handsome device made of silver and inlaid with mother-of-pearl. Yuby gave a pleasant nod, and the gaudily dressed Frenchman went back to work. No one else paid Yuby much mind. Black cowboys were not so rare, after all. That, mused Wellman, was one good thing about the frontier. Most times, with most folk, it didn't matter what *color* man you were, but rather what *kind* of man you were.

The faro table was doing brisk trade. There were four drovers bunched around the spread. Yuby watched the dealer face up the pair of Hart's Linen Eagles drawn from the dealing box. A deuce and a seven-spot. Jean Claude moved the ivories in the casekeeper. One cowboy had lost on the deuce, another had won on the seven; the others checked the casekeeper and the spread and wondered whether to let their bets on other numbers ride for the next play.

"Care to place a small wager, *m'sieu?*" Jean Claude asked Wellman.

Yuby said, "I don't take chances."

Then he pushed off the wall, for Carson was now working his way over to the table run by Lee Stanhouse....

The first hand that Stanhouse dealt Carson contained a pair of tens. The gambler provided the next man with a pair of queens so that he could open, and gave the waddy on his right four diamonds. He dealt himself the first of the three nines he had stacked for himself. There was a third queen on the bottom for the cowboy directly across the table. Stanhouse wanted to see how the betting went before deciding whether to feed out that third lady and give the cowboy facing him the winning hand. He passed to Carson, who passed to the man with the openers. The two dollar bet came around to Carson, and Carson folded. That caught Stanhouse by surprise. The newcomer acted like he had come for some reason other than poker. Stanhouse bottom-dealt the third queen and let the second cowboy win.

On the next deal Stanhouse gave Carson a pair of kings, one of them a club, and three more clubs to round out the hand, one designed to test Carson's poker instincts. Carson gave his cards only a cursory look. Stanhouse passed to him, and Carson opened for a dollar. Stanhouse didn't like it. The hand had potential and was worth a better opening wager.

When it came time for cards the waddy hesitated, for Stanhouse had dealt him a pair of sixes and an ace. Lee knew the man would hold the ace and discard two. The gambler had a third six-spot placed to reward the cowboy with three of a kind if he threw away the ace. Otherwise the third six would fill out his own straight. To Stanhouse the ace was just another card; to most cowboys it was a thing of magic.

While they waited for the cowboy to make up his mind, Carson stared at Stanhouse so intently that the gambler finally smiled, a bit rigidly, and asked, "Do I know you, sir? I have the vague idea that we have met before."

"They say I resemble my brother some," replied Carson.

The old trail hand, exasperated with his own indecision, finally threw out two discards. Stanhouse gave up one and dealt himself the six, drawing to an inside straight and, of course, filling it. Ordinarily this might have been a source of secret amusement for him, but his senses were keyed to Carson, who was still watching him.

"I believe you opened, sir," Stanhouse reminded him, polite but not friendly. "It's your bet."

Carson fattened the pot with two dollars. He had kept the kings, and Lee had not improved the pair with the draw.

"We've never met," remarked Carson. "But you knew my brother."

The other two players met Carson's bet. Stanhouse raised it by ten.

"I meet many people in my line of work."

"His name was Murdoch Kane. Remember now?"

Stanhouse's pale features were expressionless.

"That's ten more to you."

Carson called. The other two folded. Stanhouse laid out his straight and pulled in the pot. He stacked his winnings neatly, deep in thought. Everyone anted up. Stanhouse shuffled and dealt. He gave Carson five hearts and bottom-dealt an ace to himself, and after he did that he looked around the table and finally found what he was searching for in the older trail hand's face—an expression of shock and disbelief.

"Well?" His challenge was soft and fierce. "Don't you know what you saw?"

The waddy stared a him like he was a ghost.

"I pass," said Stanhouse, and swung his gaze to Carson, who was studying his flush with disinterest. The gambler saw that the young man's rough hands were trembling ever so slightly.

"How much will you open for, sir?" pressed Stanhouse, his civility an obvious farce.

Carson didn't look up at Stanhouse as he put a dollar in the pot.

Stanhouse shook his head. "A flush merits more confidence," he chided.

The cowboy across from Stanhouse gave Carson a wide-eyed look.

"What did he say?" he asked thickly.

"You may as well throw in your hand," Stanhouse advised, his tone contemptuous and raw-edged. "Those two treys are all you are going to get this go-round."

"You goddamned cheat," muttered the waddy with hostile wonder, rising up slowly on the gambler's right.

Stanhouse had one hand below the table now.

Carson put down his cards and leaned forward.

Over at the bar, Grady had traded the wooden marker for his gun and shellbelt. Lon watched him strap on the rig. Grady was wearing a tight, crazy little smile.

"Are we leaving?" mumbled Lon, his thought-processes dulled by whiskey.

125

"One way or the other."

"What's up?"

"Everything," breathed Grady, devil-may-care.

At the table, with his sad eyes hooded now, Lee Stanhouse smiled faintly at Carson and said, "Death has come a-knocking."

Chapter Fifteen

Most of the men in The Palace were blissfully unaware that calamity was lurking in their midst until Grady Harmon, his voice pitched higher than normal, cried out, "This is for Murdoch Kane, you lowdown bastard!" That exclamation turned heads, and almost everyone stopped what they were doing to watch Grady. A trail hand at the bar froze with a shot glass of whiskey held halfway between mahogany and mouth. A winner at a table where three-card monte was played became immobilized leaning over the table with his arms embracing the stakes. It wasn't until Grady, walking stiffly toward Stanhouse's table, yanked his revolver from its holster that chaos erupted. There was a general and violently determined effort to get to the rear of the saloon, as escape through the front doors was blocked by imminent gunplay. Against this strong current of self-preservation two men pushed forward: Yuby Wellman and Clyde Hobart, the latter emerging from the door to his office.

Lee Stanhouse stood up. His demeanor was calm and composed as he watched Grady coming at him. Carson saw the Sharps derringer, an ivory-handled .22 caliber over-and-under, in the gambler's right hand, and the hand stayed down at Lee's side even as Grady, his shooting arm locked rigidly straight, brought his own gun up in a jerky motion and fired. He was no

127

more than fifteen feet from his target, but he missed all the same. Stanhouse felt the wind of the passing slug on his cheek, and heard it slap into the wall behind him. A peculiar smile touched his lips, and Carson thought he looked almost apologetic as he lifted his right arm in a slow and graceful sweep. The little hideout was all but hidden in his grasp.

Stanhouse fired. The Sharps derringer cracked, a lightweight percussion compared to the shocking boom of Grady's .44 hogleg. Grady seemed to throw his head back violently. He took two steps forward and then his knees buckled. His gun arm slowly descended. A dying convulsion triggered his second shot. Splinters flew as the bullet cratered the floor. Then Grady did a slow, tilting pirouette, and as the life went out of him his body crumpled and struck the floor with a dead thump.

Lon Banks, numb with shock, pushed away from the bar and shuffled over to Grady's body, moving like a sleepwalker. He looked at the blackened hole in his best friend's forehead with uncomprehending eyes. Grady's eyes were open and full of surprise, but they looked right through Lon, focusing on something mysterious and faraway.

Carson jumped clumsily to his feet, overturning his chair. The older trail hand was pressed up against the front window, out of the line of fire, and the other drover, the one who had been sitting directly between Grady and Stanhouse, had dived to the floor the moment the gambler raised the derringer. He lay there, quite still, belly down and quite uninclined for the time being to move a hair. Carson was reaching around under his coat when Stanhouse pinned him with a fever-bright gaze.

"I know you have a gun back there," said the gambler quietly. "Don't let me see it."

But Carson failed to heed that subtle warning. He was confused and so wretchedly afraid that his animal instincts for survival compelled him to at least have a gun in hand. He had no express purpose. He wasn't bent on shooting Stanhouse, but at the same time a tiny voice—reason—warned him that the gambler might not know this.

And then strong arms clasped him from behind, pinning his arms tightly to his sides. Carson fought the strong embrace, gasping with fear. But Yuby Wellman lifted his boots off the floor and turned him around. In this way the Triangle foreman shielded Carson from Stanhouse with his own body. Yuby gave the cardsharp a steady and dauntless look.

"He's out of the game," he said.

Stanhouse took this as a promise on the part of the black cowboy, sensing immediately that Wellman did not intend to pose a threat, and nodded.

Lon Banks slipped slowly to his knees beside Grady Harmon's body and reached out to shake Grady's shoulder very gently. "Grady? Grady?" He called the name several more times, a lost entreaty.

Clyde Hobart broke free of the press of grim onlookers and looked down at the dead man, then at Lon. His gaze lifted across to Lee Stanhouse and gave the gambler a full dose of anger followed by resignation. Then a gruff, anxious voice behind him said a flat "Watch out," and Hobart's attention swung back to Lon, who was prying the gun from Grady's hand.

"Don't do that," pleaded Hobart. "You're a fool if you do that."

But Lon didn't hear him. He moved as in a dream, unhurried and methodical. He wasn't looking vengeful or full of hate, he just looked ruined. He stood up, swaying unsteadily, and Clyde Hobart took a hasty backward step, just as the front doors of The Palace burst open. Carried in on a frigid gust of wind that sent the pasteboards fluttering from Stanhouse's table came Irish Joe Kempen. Everybody looked at him, everybody but Lon Banks and Lee Stanhouse. Irish saw the dead man first, and then the gun coming up in both of Lon's hands. With a long stride he closed in and swung his stick hard, connecting with Lon's wrists. The gun clattered on the floor. Irish kept moving, and with an outswung elbow caught Lon in the sternum and dropped him. Lon looked up at him, bewildered, then crawled for the gun. Irish stared with a kind of sickened wonder. "Leave it alone," he advised harshly, but Lon kept crawling, gathered up the gun, his movements clumsy, and got back on his feet. Irish was waiting for that and swung the stick again. An ugly murmur rippled through the crowd of trail hands as the stick crashed against Lon's neck, just below the right ear. Lon's eyes rolled up in his head and he dropped like a poleaxed steer.

Irish turned on Hobart. "No trouble in your place, huh?" His words were savage and merciless. "What the hell happened?"

Hobart grew defiant. It sounded to him like Irish was blaming him for the shooting. Worse, he had a hunch that he *was* to blame, at least partially. Again he looked over at Stanhouse, who was standing behind his table with an unassailable and undaunted loftiness, as though he were disdainful of mere mortals and their tragedies. Hobart thought he saw right through Stanhouse's genteel refinement then; for the first time he saw the gambler for what he was—a cheat and a murderer.

"Ask him," Hobart snapped.

Irish glanced at Stanhouse, who now watched Hobart with faint condescension.

"I'll tell you what happened," said the older trail hand at the front window, the man Lee had permitted to see the bottom deal. "This tinhorn runs a crooked game. We caught him at it and he pulled that hideout."

"You caught me at it," laughed Stanhouse, contemptuous.

The waddy's attention was drawn to the derringer in the gambler's fist. Stanhouse was holding it down at his side, unthreatening, but the cowboy felt imperiled all the same. He could visualize the cartridge waiting in the second barrel. He could see it very clearly.

"I'll take your gun," Irish told Stanhouse.

"Don't you want to know who fired first?" asked Stanhouse impudently.

Irish had heard the gunshots, the boom of the .44 followed

by the crack of the Sharps. He knew what had happened just as certainly as if he had been an eyewitness.

"I know," he replied. "You're coming with me."

"Leave him to us," came a loud and insistent cry from somewhere in the congregation of cowboys."

"Yeah, that's the way it's done," called another.

"You don't steal a man's horse and you don't cheat him at cards."

"You do and you forfeit your life!"

Suddenly almost everyone was talking, angry muttering exchanges, and the crowd began to move restlessly.

"He killed one of ours," someone shouted. "They're just trying to protect him. That ain't no way to see justice done!"

One of the trail hands leaned over the bar and told one of the aprons truculently, "Gimme my gun."

Hobart turned around. The barkeep looked to him for orders, and Hobart shook his head.

"Back off, mister," the apron advised the cowboy.

"Go to hell," growled the drover. He started clambering over the bar. The barkeep socked him in the jaw. The cowboy slithered down the front of the counter. Several punchers swore, and then the whole belligerent mass surged at the mahogany. Half a dozen of them scaled the ramparts. The aprons reached for the sawed-off shotguns spaced under the counter, but they were outnumbered and swiftly overwhelmed. Hobart went down, rabbit-punched. Irish moved toward Stanhouse. He didn't see Patch Russell come over the threshold behind him. One of the first cowboys over the bar grabbed up his shellbelt and then got back on the mahogany. He had the belt in one hand, his gun in the other. His back was to Russell and he was yelling at the crowd, and though his exhortation was lost in the crashing tumult his meaning was not, for he pointed at Stanhouse. He pointed his gun. He wasn't aiming, he wasn't even looking that way, but Russell swung his Davenport 10-gauge up and fired full choke from the hip. The double-ought buckshot caught the trail hand in the back of the head and between the shoulder blades. The impact picked him up and then slammed him face-down on the bar. He slid a good ten feet, leaving a smear of blood from nose and mouth. The whole crew froze. Irish spun and stared at Patch. Russell broke open the Davenport and reached into the side pocket of his coat for fresh shells. He acted casual, like a man out in a field hunting quail. Irish uttered a strangled growl and lunged. He put all his strength behind the stick that came up and smashed into Patch's face. Russell cakewalked backwards and dropped the shotgun. He sat down hard in the doorway, leaned forward from the waist. Blood was spewing from his ruined mouth to puddle between his splayed legs.

The cry went up then, a wild and savage and fearsome cry that seemed to shake the whole building.

Carson Kane began to fight against Yuby's hold with new fervor. Wellman wrenched the boy's arm up at a painful angle and applied pressure sufficient to persuade Carson to release his hold on the gun. The revolver fell to the floor and Yuby kicked it away. It skittered under Stanhouse's table. The waddy turned the table over and dove for it. Stanhouse took one step back and placed himself against the wall, raising the derringer slightly. On hands and knees, the old trail hand looked up and into the barrels of the Sharps. Carson's gun lay under his left hand and he was seeing that cartridge again, vividly.

"Your play," rasped Stanhouse.

The crowd surged forward. Most of them were still unarmed. The barkeeps were scuffling, swarmed by drovers. But the rest of the cowboys wanted to get their hands on Stanhouse or Russell or both. Their faces were flushed with an ugly poison. They had to go through Irish. Kempen felt as though everything had come apart. By shooting the cowboy on the bar, Russell had somehow robbed him of his edge, his confidence, his sense to being in the right. He faltered mentally, and the men coming at him saw this momentary weakness, this lack of conviction, and seized the advantage. One picked up an overturned deal chair and swung it at Kempen. Irish surrendered to certain failure, certain pain, put his head down and went in under the chair. A half-dozen punchers closed in on him, and he went down under battering blows, blinded by his own blood, flailing ruthlessly with his big fists.

Clem Brackett stepped in out of the night.

He spared Patch Russell the briefest glance as he got by the injured deputy. The Remington was in his hand. He aimed it at the ceiling and put two holes in the green tin. The tide of cowboys halted. He swept the front rank with cold gray eyes. The frigid wind blustered in through the doorway and pushed against his back. His two shots had stilled all the action, just as had happened when Russell unloaded the buckshot into the back of the man he had bushwhacked. Brackett stood there confronted by twenty-odd contentious, blood-lusting Texans . . . and he smiled. It was a flinty, godless smile. It hit the trail hands with more force than the gunshots he had thrown skyward.

Brackett singled out one of the men in the forefront. This one was carrying his shellbelt in his left hand and had his right on the butt of his still-holstered gun. Brackett put away the Remington and walked right at the man. The bunch that had beset Irish stepped away from the deputy. Irish was on one knee, his head drooping, shirt torn, his face and the knuckles of his hands covered with blood. Brackett paid him no attention. He focused on his target and he didn't slow his stride as he closed in, so that the cowboy reflexively stepped back to avoid impact. Only then did Brackett stop. He was still sporting that half-wild smile.

"Drop it," he said.

Subdued, the man relinquished his hold on gun and belt. These fell with a thump to the floor at Brackett's feet, like an offering to some pagan god.

"Get up, Joe," Brackett demanded, without taking his gaze

from the man he had walked down.

"I *am* getting up," snapped Irish thickly, lifting unsteadily to his feet.

"The cardsharp killed one of ours," muttered the man facing Brackett. It was an explanation, of sorts.

"Shut up," said Brackett flatly. He turned abruptly and set a course that took him along the front edge of the crowd, so close that all along the line the trail hands had to give ground to avoid contact. This brought him close to Stanhouse's overturned table. Brackett considered Yuby and Carson, and then the gambler against the wall, and finally the puncher on hands and knees amongst the whiskey-splattered cards and cash and coin.

"On your feet," Brackett told this one. "And leave the gun there."

"If I move that, sonuvabitch will plug me with that damned hideout."

Brackett peered speculatively at Stanhouse. "No, he won't. Because I'll kill him where he stands if he tries."

Stanhouse let his gunarm drop down by his side.

"Are you coming with me?" Brackett asked him, "Or staying here with them?"

Stanhouse surveyed the crowd of cowboys without apprehension.

"It doesn't matter to me. But it does to you, I suppose."

"Irish," Brackett drawled, "take him out."

Kempen found his stick, and Stanhouse made for the doorway, his head high, his gait unhurried. Irish fell in behind. Patch looked dazedly at Kempen as he went by and opened his mouth, a gaping toothless bloody hole, but all that emerged was a grunt. Irish resisted the urge to kick Russell out into the street and passed on into the night. He had never felt such disgust for someone, or so sour on life. Brackett came over and assisted Russell to his feet, but Patch's knees had turned to jelly and Brackett had to stay with him to keep him upright. He gave the trail hands a final look.

"This place is closed. I want all of you out of Two Rivers. Right now. I want you to go quiet. Don't make me come back down here."

With that he gave them his back, and half-carried Russell out of The Palace.

Chapter Sixteen

Doc Milby was waiting for them on the boardwalk of the jail, displaying the stern disapproval of a father who has caught his boys doing wrong. His hair was mussed, for he had just turned in when the shooting started. Descending from his office-cum-living quarters above McKaskle's store, he had proceeded immediately down Main, grip in hand, and had seen the procession strung out along Smoke and heading north toward him.

Stanhouse was in the lead, with the carefree stride of a ne'er-do-well out for an evening stroll. He mounted the boardwalk, gave Milby a pleasant nod and an amicable "Good evening," and proceeded on into the jail. Irish was next. His attitude was truculent and he was swinging his stick like he wanted very much to use it on somebody. Milby noted the blood on his bruised face and torn shirt and scraped hands. Behind Irish a good twenty paces came Patch Russell. Russell walked like a man who couldn't plant a firm step or walk a straight line for anything. His jaw was slacked open as though the muscles that worked it had been cut, and his blood-smeared face was already swelling. Sticking close to Russell was Brackett. A short distance from The Palace Russell had shaken loose the marshal's helping hands, but Brackett had remained near at hand, prepared to catch the deputy should he stumble and fall.

137

Bringing up the rear of the train was Brackett's sorrel. It had been trained to follow Brackett if he set out on foot, unless tethered.

As Irish went by Milby said, "Who's hurt the worst?"

Kempen thumbed over his shoulder, indicating Patch, without breaking stride.

"He is. But not bad enough."

"Let me help you," offered the sawbones as Patch came within reach, but Russell wrenched his arm free of Milby's grasp and stalked inside.

Brackett hitched the sorrel to a tie rail, mounted the boardwalk, and paused to look down the length of Smoke. There were men in the street now, both mounted and afoot, and their activity raised a storm of dust that was whipped into the sky by the relentless gusts. The stars and the moon were gone now, the sky black as pitch. Brackett watched the distant drovers closely for a long moment. He could hear voices raised and the thunder of galloping horses, but the riders were going south. Back to the herd camps. He expected things to quiet down on the Texas Side in a big hurry tonight. But tomorrow, that was the question. He knew it wasn't over. Two Texas boys were dead. There would almost certainly be hell to pay.

"Didn't figure on seeing you out tonight," remarked Milby.

Brackett turned to him. "Why not? This is where I'm supposed to be. Same as you."

Over Milby's shoulder he could spy a cluster of figures on the boardwalk on The Plainsman. Closer, a man was hustling toward the jail along the boardwalks of the buildings on the north side of Main. Brackett couldn't tell in the darkness who it was and he didn't much care. Whoever it was looked like trouble, but not gun trouble.

With Milby at his heels Brackett went inside. Stanhouse was standing over by the cellblock door. The door was open and the gambler was looking in at the cells like a sightseer. Irish had taken the swivel chair behind the desk. Sprawled back, he held his head low and stared at Patch, who was just inside the front door, swaying slightly, clenching and unclenching his hands.

"Sit down before you fall down," Milby told Patch curtly.

Russell shuffled over to a ladderback chair in the corner, where he could keep an eye on Irish. Milby bent down to make a close examination of what had once been Russell's mouth.

"God in heaven, man," breathed Milby, shaking his head. "What happened to you?"

"I did," muttered Irish, and then he looked at Brackett, a defiant I-told-you-so look that gave Brackett a clue as to what had transpired in The Palace prior to his timely arrival.

Brackett turned to Stanhouse. "Take your pick. The doors are unlocked. And I'll take the hideout. I told you once. This will be the last time."

Stanhouse surrendered the Sharps derringer. Brackett slipped it into his coat pocket. With impregnable dignity the gambler entered the cellblock. Brackett followed. There were four cells, two on either side of a short hall, no windows, and one door, barred and bolted, at the back. Stanhouse selected the first cell on the left. He closed the door himself. The cage was furnished with a wooden bench, long enough and wide enough to sleep on. A brown wool blanket was rolled up at one end. A wooden pail was shoved up under the bench.

"What exactly are the charges, Marshal?"

"I'm not charging you, mister. I'm just holding you. The circuit judge will decide what charges, if any, are brought against you."

"I suspect those Texans will want to have a say in that."

"Too bad for them."

"You have a lot of sand," said Stanhouse with admiration. "I was impressed by the way you handled yourself. You walk right up to death and spit in its eye."

Brackett turned to go.

Stanhouse said, "Don't forget to lock this door, Marshal."

"Don't jackrabbit on me," warned Brackett. "It'll tick me off."

Back in the office he saw that Irish was absent. Milby was

tending to Patch, his grip open and in Russell's lap. A quick thumping of bootheels on the boardwalk announced the arrival of the man Brackett had seen highballing down Main. He heard McKaskle say, breathlessly, "I heard the gunfire all the way up Fremont. What happened?" And then Irish was speaking, a curt response. "Clem's in the office." McKaskle charged inside. The merchant was a narrow, bony man. He was bald on top, with thick wings of jet-black hair on the sides. His eyes were big, bulging in their sockets like they just did not fit his head. They reminded Brackett of the eyes of Kiowa children, impoverished and undernourished, that he had witnessed outside the gates of Fort McPherson at the tail end of hard winters. McKaskle had thrown on his trousers and shin boots and a clawhammer coat over the top of his long johns.

"Clem," he gasped, his cheeks reddened by the bleak night and the exertion of his long run from his nice home up Fremont. "I heard the shots. What happened?"

Brackett was in no mood for interference, from McKaskle or anybody else.

"What are you doing, Leon? Go home."

McKaskle ruffled. "I am a councilman, Marshal. What goes on in Two Rivers is my concern. And you work for me, remember?"

Brackett had the urge to quit right then and there, to take the star off his shirt and pitch it at McKaskle. But he knew he couldn't, not and live with himself. He had to see this through, and if his perception of the Texas cowboy mentality was on the mark, the trouble was far from being over. Pride, he thought, was a real handicap for someone interested in long life.

"Yeah," he said sourly. "I remember."

"So?"

"There was an altercation over a game of cards at The Palace. One of Hobart's gamblers shot and killed a drover."

"And Russell shot another," said Irish, standing in the doorway. "Shot him in the back, by the way."

McKackle pivoted and gaped at Kempen. There was a brief

scuffle over in the corner, Russell grunting something unintelligible and Milby snapping at him to shut up and sit still.

"This was bound to happen," sighed McKaskle woefully. "You play with fire and you get burned. In fact, this isn't the first time. It happened before. Two or three years ago."

"Not quite like this," persisted Irish. "This time a deputy town marshal shot a trail hand in the back."

McKaskle scowled. "Yes. You told me that once already."

"The gambler is Lee Stanhouse," said Brackett mildly. "The same one who killed Murdoch Kane two years ago. That time it was self-defense, or so I understand, and this time, if I read it right, it was also self-defense. A rancher by the name of Tyler Kane came up here with the intention of shooting Stanhouse, because Murdock Kane was his boy."

"How do you come by this information?"

Brackett didn't feel like explaining about Sigel's confessional to Magruder, or Daybreak's bringing the word to him. So he said, "Just take my word for it."

McKaskle brushed past Brackett and went to the cellblock doorway. He fixed a detesting glare on Stanhouse, who was leaning against the iron bars with his arms folded across his chest.

"You and your kind are nothing but trouble," he sneered.

"You need us," said Stanhouse impudently, "so that you can feel that you're better."

McKaskle returned to Brackett. "I'm going to call a meeting of the council in the morning. I want you to be there, Marshal. I will move that we pass an ordinance that will call for you to close down the Texas Side once and for all."

"So Mac was right," mused Brackett.

"What was that?"

"Nothing."

"We have come to the point where we must decide the future of Two Rivers," persisted McKaskle, raising his voice to the ringing level of oratory. "Good, honest, hardworking people are pouring into this country. They want to make this town a safe, solid, and prosperous community. A good place to live. A good place to raise children. We don't need Little Texas or desperate characters like that cardsharp in there. Let the Texas cattlemen take their herds elsewhere. Close down the Texas Side, Marshal. Drive out the bad element."

"The railroad may not like it," remarked Brackett, an indifferent devil's advocate. "They make money freighting beeves."

"They make more money bringing out the homesteaders. Don't worry about the railroaders."

"I'm not worried."

Irish laughed, soft and derisive. "You two. You just don't see it, do you? You don't have to bother about closing down the Texas Side. After what happened tonight they'll like as not put the whole bloody town to the torch."

McKaskle stared blankly at him. "Why would they do that?" He sounded this side of apprehensive.

"I told you why twice," barked Kempen.

"Do you think they'd dare?" McKaskle asked Brackett.

"Those men will dare anything," shrugged Brackett. "We'll have to wait and see."

"I won't." Irish went to the desk and put his hand on it. When the hand came away Brackett saw the tin star lying there. He didn't want to look Kempen in the eye, but he forced himself to do so.

"You think I'm running out on you," declared Irish. "Well, I shouldn't have to. You shouldn't even be here, Clem. And I want no part of a law that shoots a man in the back. I think it's high time I went back to honest work."

Kempen walked out. McKaskle examined the expression on Brackett's face and got a strong impulse to leave as well.

"I'll see you tomorrow, Marshal," he said, and was quickly gone.

Brackett slowly shut the door. He went to each of the front windows in turn and closed the shutters, dropping the cross bars down to secure them. The shutters were fashioned from two-inch thick beams of hickory. Each one had a lateral gunport cut into it. Then he moved to the gun rack on the wall behind the desk and freed a Winchester 44/40 from the chain. He took a box of ammunition from a desk drawer—fifty solid head, center fire bullets. As he sat on the corner of the desk, loading the repeater, he sent a single glance across the room. Russell had been watching him past Doc Milby's bulk, and now quickly avoided Brackett's eyes.

Chapter Seventeen

It was a gray morning, bitter and bleak, the clouds reaching from horizon to horizon, their bellies dark and pregnant with sleet and snow, the wind unrelenting. Banjo Stubbins had taken the tarpaulin down during the night for fear of losing it. He was hunkered down upwind of the cookfire, hunching his back against the wintry gale and holding his hands out close to the dancing flames, when the Triangle crew came back into camp. Nine riders, with Tyler Kane in the lead, a grim and silent cavalcade. The steam of exhalation clouded the faces of men and horses. They had all gone to pay their last respects to Grady Harmon, put under at dawn in Two Rivers' boot hill. Only a pair of herd guards and one of the *remuda* wranglers stayed behind with Banjo.

The horsemen dismounted and tied their ponies to a tether rope strung between two cottonwoods, then gathered near the big fire out a ways from the chuckwagon. Banjo had maintained it during their absence, along with the smaller blaze near which he now squatted. Stubbins watched them closely, plumbing the collective mood. Hardly a word passed among them as they tried to thaw frozen limbs. A close bond had developed between these men who had been through so much together, and Grady had been one of them. They were taciturn characters as a rule, more inclined to demonstrate their feelings through action than word. And Banjo knew the action they were thinking about taking now bode ill for the man who had shot Grady Harmon.

Worst hit of them all was Lon Banks. He sat over by the cutbank, away from the fire and from the others, pulling his knees up against his chest and wrapping his arms around his legs and staring like a lost soul at the ground in front of him. The other hands were painfully aware of his special, private misery, but they left him alone, for they had no skill with words of comfort that might lessen grief.

Tyler Kane gave it a try, though, and Banjo watched as he knelt and spoke to Banks, but Lon just gave him a blank and forlorn look before returning to his contemplation of the dust. Banjo's attention was diverted to Carson, who was striding across the camp toward the chuckwagon. Anger sharpened his every movement. Yuby Wellman left the tether rope and came after him. Carson did not bother with the custom of asking the cook's permission before undoing one of the wagon tarp tiedowns and reaching into the bed of the Studebaker. When he came out with the Henry repeater Banjo stood up in a hurry. Only once during the push had there been a need for the rifles to come out of his keeping, when the hidehunters had rimwalked the herd along the upper Brazos. Carson going for the rifle meant he had killing work in mind.

Carson turned right into Yuby and made a step around, but Wellman grabbed the rifle where barrel met breech with one hand. Carson tried to wrench the Henry free, but all his strength and purpose could not even straighten Wellman's arm.

"Stay out of my way," snarled Carson furiously. "You manhandled me last night like I was some greenhorn kid. Well, I was raised on short grass, and by God I'll fight you if you try that again."

"You talk like a man," said Yuby evenly, "now why don't you try to act like one?"

This incensed Carson to the point of frenzy. He started

tussling with Wellman, trying to jerk the foreman off balance and twist the rifle free all at once. Everybody looked over, but Tyler Kane did more than that; he came charging across camp like a bull ready to hook something. He was of a mind to take issue with anyone and anything—a man pushed as far as he was going to be pushed.

Yuby let go of the repeater when he saw how far Carson was willing to go, and Carson stumbled backwards, fetching up against the side of the chuckwagon. He pushed off and went straight into Tyler's stiff-arm, which drove him back again, and pinned him there. He gave his father a surly look, gripping the Henry so fiercely that his knuckles were white.

"Where do you think you're going?" demanded Kane.

"To finish what I should've finished last night in that saloon."

"What the hell has gotten into you, boy?"

"I plan to do what you should have done in the first place," challenged Carson scornfully. "So the world will know that there's at least one Kane who has the grit to do what has to be done."

"Oh, you were going to shoot that gambler, were you? Lon told me all about it. How you went in there with your iron under your coat like a damned assassin. How you got Grady to point Stanhouse out. And how you bought into Stanhouse's game. So what was your plan, exactly? Just introduce yourself and then pull out that hideout, put it to the man's head and pull the trigger? They would've hanged you for sure. It would've been murder, clear-cut."

"You're one to talk about murder!" exploded Carson.

Kane took a step back and dropped his arm, releasing Carson.

"I let Reese go last night. I told him the deal was off."

Carson didn't say anything for a moment. It was all he could handle just digesting the implications of that disclosure. Tyler looked at Wellman.

"Does that surprise you?" Kane asked the foreman.

Yuby shook his head. "Your hiring him in the first place is what surprised me."

"Let's just say I forgot who I was. I was too wrapped up in what I had become. Or *thought* I had become. I thought I was a man who was above the law, but I forgot that there is a law besides the one you find in a judge's book. An unwritten law that was all we had to live by before the judges and the lawyers and the courts came out this far. A law that says a man whose son has been gunned down must give like for like. That if you feel you have been wronged then you should balance the scales. But that law also says that you must do it yourself, and damn the consequences."

"I couldn't bring myself to see it through," muttered Carson miserably. "I told Stanhouse who I was. When I mentioned Murdoch's name it was like he thought it over and decided it was time to die. Like he was living in hell, and so tired of living. I actually felt sorry for him, somehow. Ain't that a laugh? But the fact is I started it all last night. I roped Grady into it. And if I'd done what I'd set out to do then Grady wouldn't be dead. So instead of solving anything I just made things worse."

"Speaking of which," murmured Banjo, and they all followed his gaze.

Another bunch of riders was coming into the Triangle camp, ten men in long coats with hatbrims pulled low over ruthless, hard-set features—men on a mission. In the lead was a wiry little man with a sweeping mustache and a gray goatee wearing a white slicker. Banjo could tell immediately that these men were cowboys by trade, but they weren't riding on cowboy work this day. Every saddle scabbard sported a rifle.

The horsemen pulled up at the rim of the camp, and the man in the white slicker brought his Palouse a bit closer to the chuckwagon before dismounting. He came at Kane peeling the glove from his right hand and offered his hand to Tyler.

"Colonel Riley Davis, sir. These are my boys. We haven't met, but I've heard tell of you, Kane."

Kane grasped his hand. "And I you, Colonel. The RD Connected."

The formalities performed, Davis put his glove back on and moodily watched his fingers as he flexed them.

"I got the word that one of your men was killed last night in Little Texas. So was one of mine. Shot in the back with a sawed-off. We took him out and buried him in the wild wide-open. Too many honest cowboys are planted in that damn town's graveyard already. I'm of a mind today to fill it up with locals."

Kane's eyes narrowed. "What are you suggesting, Colonel?"

"My boys and I are riding into Two Rivers today. We're gonna even things once and for certain. I want the sonuvabitch that drygulched my man. These man have voted on it. They say they can't turn their backs and go back home with tail twixt legs. It's high time we taught these people that they can't ride a Texan roughshod and not get throwed."

The Triangle crew was edging closer, hanging on every word. The warmth of the fire was forgotten. A hotter fire was blazing in their chests, fanned by the colonel's inflammatory talk. It was clear they didn't need a vote.

"From what I hear," said Kane, "the man you're after is one of the lawmen."

Davis snorted. "A badge don't give him the right to do what he did. And it won't protect him from our brand of justice. If we don't do something, nobody will. Spittin' in the street is a worse crime in Two Rivers than killing a Texan. You should know, Kane."

Kane didn't answer, but Lon Banks shoved out in front of the cluster of Triangle cowboys, quick to speak up.

"I'm with you, Colonel!" he cried, raising a defiant fist.

"The law in Two Rivers protects the cheats and cutthroats on the Texas Side," exclaimed Davis, addressing the Triangle crew directly now. "It's not a just law. It sure isn't our law. We bring our own. It is hard and quick and merciless, but it is fair."

"And what if they don't give up that lawman?" asked Yuby.

Davis turned on Wellman. It was apparent that he would brook no nay-saying.

"Then we take him. We'll burn the Texas Side to the ground if we have to. We'll put the whole corrupt, miserable town to the torch." He gave Kane a challenging look. "What have we got to lose? They damn near stole our herds from us this year. That's bad enough. But they step over the line when they start gunning down our boys."

"Yes," said Kane, his resolve hardening. "What *have* we got left to lose? Except our pride if we let it stand and just ride away." He faced his men. "Well, boys? What's it going to be?"

They did not whoop or holler their feelings. They only moved as one, with a grim unity of purpose, toward the line of horses under cottonwoods that were whipped into a rustling frenzy by the blustery norther.

"Break out the long guns, Banjo," Kane told Stubbins.

"Do it your own self," barked the old cook belligerently.

Kane stared at Banjo like he couldn't believe his own ears.

"Don't start on me with your holier-than-thou horse shit," warned Banjo. "I won't be a party to this, and if you try to crowd me you'll have more of a fight than you can handle right here, *Mister* Kane."

Kane hesitated but Lon Banks didn't. He rushed forward, unfastened a couple more tie-downs, and got up under the wagon tarp to bring out the rifles two by two. Once mounted, the Triangle boys came by single-file and Banks handed out the artillery. One of the others brought up his horse, and Banks swung eagerly up into the saddle. Another had Yuby's claybank in tow. Wellman took the offered reins, but then led the horse over to the wagon and hitched it to a wheel.

"Aren't you riding with us, Yuby?" asked one of the Triangle hands, worried.

Yuby looked up into their dark, ruddy faces, and then at Kane. Tyler was edgy. He knew that Wellman had strong influence with his men. They all respected the foreman and looked to him for leadership. Yuby was the one man who could challenge the authority of Tyler Kane, the one man who could dissuade the hands from following their boss. The man who could steal the loyalty of the crew from Kane.

Wellman knew this. He could make a stand, argue his case and, if he won, break Kane. And that, he concluded, was something he could never do. Kane's stance and expression were a summons to combat. Out of respect, Yuby did not pick up the gauntlet.

"I told you I didn't want any part of this," he said, "but you pulled me in, all the same. So now I'm getting out. It's either that or stand against you."

"Go ahead," sneered Kane. "You seem to have this idea that you're a better man. You have a way about you that has rubbed me wrong for quite a spell. I should have cut you down a notch or two a long time ago."

Wellman stood very still, saying nothing else but not turning away, either. It was Kane who broke the standoff, doing it with reproach, addressing Carson bluntly.

"Mount up, boy. We'll finish this together and finish it right."

Carson dared to glance uncertainly at Wellman, a silent petition for guidance. Yuby had never failed to counsel him wisely. But now Wellman returned his gaze with the impassivity of an uncaring stranger. Kane was provoked to unreasoning wrath. In this blinding storm of rage he struck Carson across the face with an open hand. Carson slammed back against the side of the wagon once more. He was startled more than hurt. His shock became humiliation, and the humiliation became hostility.

"I knew you'd never amount to half the man your brother was," growled Kane.

"That tears it!" bellowed Banjo, charging forward to stand between father and son. He stood nose-to-nose with Kane, so thoroughly incensed that he shook from head to toe. "You ignorant old fool! Somebody oughta put a bullet in your brainpan and call it a cent and a half well spent. You don't deserve a son like Carson, *Mister* Kane. Murdoch, maybe. I don't recollect having ever met a more worthless cuss in all my born days. He had the eyes of a coyote and a nature to match. He was a braggart and a bully and a liar. Now I know where he got those sterling qualities."

"I should kill you where you stand," breathed Kane.

"Why don't you hire somebody to do it!" sneered Stubbins.

Kane said, "You're fired."

"Too late. I already quit."

Kane turned sharply away. A moment later he was mounted and raking his spurs brutally to urge his bay into a hard gallop. Davis led the RD Connected crew after him. Lon Banks was in the vanguard of the Triangle bunch following close behind. Carson, Yuby and Banjo watched them go. Seventeen riders in all. Texas fury on horseback, bound for Two Rivers.

Chapter Eighteen

Clyde Hobart came calling at the jail in the half-light of dawn, taking short, rigid steps because of the cold. He wore a long dove-gray overcoat with its ermine-lined collar upturned, kid gloves on his hands, and a derby hat pulled down tight on his head. But for all this extra fabric he was still freezing. He kept his chin tucked until he got up onto the boardwalk of the jail. Here, at least, there was some shelter from the wintry zephyr. He looked up and for the first time saw that the windows had been shuttered. The place looked like a fortress. There was movement to be seen through the lateral gunports on the right side, and he called out, "It's Hobart. I've come to see Stanhouse. Let me in, for God's sake."

He heard the scrape of the crossbar being lifted off the door, which then swung open. Eager to get in out of the weather, Hobart took a step forward, but Brackett blocked his way. The marshal glanced past Hobart, down the empty, quiet stretch of Smoke Street, and then at the bundle under the saloon owner's arm, something wrapped in a barkeep's leather apron.

"What have you got there, Clyde?"

"Russell's greener, Marshal. I sure as hell don't want it in my possession if those Texas boys return."

"If?" Smiling dryly, Brackett put aside the Winchester /40 he had been holding loosely in his hands, and took the offering. Hobart looked relieved to be rid of it.

"You think this will save you, Clyde?" Brackett asked.

"Maybe it'll shorten the odds. Are you going to let me come inside? I'm getting frostbit out here."

Brackett stepped back. Hobart entered and went immediately to the stove, holding his hands as close as he dared to the hot iron while Brackett laid the shotgun on the desk before going back to secure the bar across the door.

"Where is Russell, anyway?" asked Hobart. Having seen firsthand what Russell was capable of, Hobart was nervous, the kind of agitation a man suffered when he knew a rabid dog was lurking somewhere in the vicinity.

Brackett nodded in the direction of the cellblock.

Hobart raised an eyebrow. "You got him locked up?"

"No, he's sleeping. The doc gave him some laudanum. Why? You figure he ought to be locked up?"

"It appeared suspiciously like cold-blooded murder to me."

"He managed to tell me that it looked to him like that cowboy was about to shoot your dealer."

"He's not my . . ." Hobart cut off the protest in mid-stride.

Brackett went to his chair, sat down and lifted a mug of coffee to his lips. He didn't even consider offering Hobart some of the java he had just boiled.

"It's a little late to wash your hands of this," mused the marshal.

"Sounds like you're accusing me of something."

"Poor judgment."

"You're one to preach. You've got a killer on your payroll."

Brackett started nudging the mug around the scarred top of the desk with his knuckles. "Maybe," he allowed. "But at the moment that's all I've got."

"Where is Kempen?"

"Pulled out."

"I'll be damned. I never thought Irish was short on . . ."

"It's not like that," snapped Brackett.

Hobart set aside his own self-pity to feel a little sorry for

Brackett. He read Clem's mind.

"You believe they'll come for Lee." It wasn't a question.

"They'll come for all of us."

Hobart put his hands on the desk and leaned forward ardently.

"Let Stanhouse go, Marshal. I'll have a fast horse waiting. Just say the word."

"Why should I do that for you, Clyde?" drawled Brackett implacably.

"For me?" Hobart barked a raw-edged laugh. "Do it for yourself."

"Those Texas boys have a bone to pick. If they don't get Stanhouse they'll take it out on you and everybody else in Little Texas. They might anyway."

Hobart was aghast. "If it comes to that you'll just hand him over? My God, Brackett. I admit I never had much good to say about you. You were forever taking pleasure from throwing your weight around south of the deadline. But I never took you for a man who would choose the safe and easy road to get anywhere."

Brackett yawned in his face. "Beg your pardon, Clyde," he said, mockingly. "It's been a long night. You can go on in and talk to your friend if you care to. You're not carrying any iron, are you?"

"Don't insult me, Marshal."

"I wouldn't think of it."

Hobart was halfway to the cellblock door when he remembered something, and glanced over his shoulder. "You say Russell's in there?"

Brackett stood up in that slow, stiff way of a man who saves his energy for the moments when he needs it most.

"I'll shake him out of it," he said, going by Hobart. "He needs to take over for me soon, anyway. I've got a town council meeting to attend." He opened the cellblock door and fastened a crooked grin on the saloon owner. "They're going to decide whether or not to run you and your *compadres* out of Two

Rivers, Clyde."

"There are other trail towns," snapped Hobart. "The services I provide may be out of favor with some, but will never be out of style."

"If you say so."

Hobart waited until Brackett came back out into the office with a groggy Patch Russell in tow. Russell glimpsed the repugnance Hobart could not disguise as the saloon owner gazed upon his damaged, grotesquely swollen face.

This, thought Hobart, *is what the bogeyman looks like, the one that folks use to scare their children into doing right.*

"Your scattergun's on the desk," Brackett told Patch, his tone none too friendly. "Compliments of Mr. Hobart here."

Russell moved unsteadily out into the office. Hobart entered the cellblock. Brackett closed the door and left him alone with Stanhouse. The gambler was sitting on the bench, the blanket draped over his shoulders.

"Well, this is an unexpected surprise," remarked Stanhouse.

Hobart drew a deep breath and took a deck of cards from the pocket of his overcoat. "I brought you something."

"Beware of Greeks bearing gifts," smiled the cardsharp. "Still being friendly to strays, eh, Clyde? Even when they bite your hand."

"I don't understand you, Lee."

Stanhouse got up and reached through the bars to take the deck of pasteboards. He gave the cards a quick, deft, one-handed shuffle.

"Why, Mr. Hobart! This is a straight deck."

"Who will you finesse now, Lee? Yourself?"

"Fate deals the cards," Stanhouse commented, sardonic. "And sometimes she will slip a joker into the play." He returned to the bench. "Sorry to be so much trouble, Clyde. But I'll be out of your hair soon enough."

Hobart choked down on his exasperation. "I want to know one thing, Lee. Guess I'm hoping you'll feel like you owe me an honest answer. What ever happened to you that has made you so sour on life?"

Stanhouse gave him a long and pensive look. Then, to Hobart's astonishment, he nodded.

"I began my, um, illustrious career in San Francisco. Oh, it was there for the taking, Clyde. The miners came in out of the gold fields like lemmings to the sea. Rondo and blackjack were the games in favor then. Poker was too slow and complicated. I got a job at the Bella Union, dealing *vingt-et-un*. For my own entertainment I would spend my leisure hours on the east side of Dupont Street."

"Chinatown," murmured Hobart.

"That's right. You won't find a people more dedicated to the pursuit of games of chance than the Chinese, Clyde, or as fair a game as *fan tan*. I met a young woman there. Her name was Tia. Her father was a *tan kun*, a *fan tan* dealer of great repute. I became . . . quite fond of Tia, and she was utterly devoted to my happiness. I even entertained the notion of marriage. She was a rare and delicate beauty, and life was a grand thing indeed."

"What happened?"

Stanhouse was staring at the deck of cards in his hand. "One afternoon we were on our way down Sacramento Street, the route from my hotel to the Bella Union. Some children set off a string of firecrackers. A team of horses spooked and a dray wagon overturned, blocking our path. Tia was beside herself with apprehension. It was bad enough, she thought, that such a thing occurred to obstruct us on our way to the gaming house. The Chinese take their superstitions seriously. But she had consulted, as was her daily custom, the *kat sing*, the book of lucky stars. The signs were not auspicious. I laughed it off.

"Back then, believe it or not, I was a straight dealer. I had never dealt a crooked hand. Tia would usually sit in a chair a little behind and to my right. She was all the edge I needed. Many of the players at my table had difficulty concentrating on the game. That evening my luck was exceptional. I just couldn't seem to lose. And the more I won the more anxious Tia became." A bitter smile touched Stanhouse's wan and melancholy face. "I recall that I said to her that with the money I had won so far that night we would be able to afford the most lavish wedding Frisco had ever seen. And then one of the miners at the table called me a cheat. I'll never forget that man, Clyde. He was a coarse, pig-eyed, brutish wretch. He pulled a gun, stood up and aimed it at me. I was so dumbfounded. I just sat there. Tia threw herself in front of me. The bullet killed her instantly." He paused, then added, grimly, "She cheated Death, you see. It came for me, and got her instead. And I have cheated at cards ever since."

Hobart finally managed to say, "I'm truly sorry, Lee. Truly sorry. But that must have been years ago."

"What does time have to do with it?" asked Stanhouse sharply.

"What happened wasn't your fault. You're not to blame for the woman's death. Why do you continue to punish yourself?"

"You still don't get it, do you? Well, it doesn't matter."

"So why do you fight?" pressed Hobart tenaciously. "Why don't you simply stand there and let them kill you?"

"I'm not sure. Maybe because every time a man calls me a cheat and pulls a gun I see that miner."

Hobart shook his head, still confused by the dark and hateful forces that moved Lee Stanhouse.

"I guess I would have to stand in your shoes and feel your feelings and live the days that make up your life to understand fully."

"You've played fair with me," Stanhouse said gratefully. "I thank you for that."

"That sounds like a goodbye."

Stanhouse did not respond. Hobart reached up and gripped the strap-iron with both hands.

"Listen," he whispered fervently. "Brackett believes those Texans will come for you. They'll either shoot you down or string you up. I can have a horse and a grubstake for you in half an hour."

"Thanks, but no. You've done enough."

"Think of others, if not of yourself. Men may try to kill one another over whether you should live or die."

"That won't be the real reason. And why should I think of others?" Stanhouse uttered a hollow and unpleasant laugh. "Such noble sentiments! Your regard for me is higher than I deserve."

Hobart stepped back. "I guess I'll never know the real Lee Stanhouse. A heartless, selfish bastard or a tragic human being? Or someone somewhere in between. But knowing would sure make things easier. For then I would know if I am right or wrong for trying to help you."

"Help yourself," recommended Stanhouse, indifferent to Hobart's dilemma.

Hobart left the cellblock. The gambler did not look up to watch his departure. Instead he dealt five cards face up onto the bench beside him. A full house. Aces and eights from the bottom of the deck. Stanhouse laughed softly.

Chapter Nineteen

Hobart trudged gloomily back down Smoke to The Palace. The glass in one of the front doors had been busted out during the previous night's fracas, and the shards crunched under his high-polished Middletons as he crossed the threshold. One of the swampers had dumped sand over the blood Patch Russell had drooled, and more sand, a larger quantity, further in where Grady Harmon had fallen. Hands shoved into the pockets of his overcoat, Hobart stood a moment and surveyed the damage with clinical detachment. The bar had been kicked in here and there. At one end the brass footrail had come loose from its moorings. The wreckage of broken chairs and tables had been swept into several piles of kindling. The trail hands had handled the furnishings with a rough and methodical malice prior to leaving. The furniture left intact was stacked up over by the north wall. One of the men he employed for cleanup was swabbing behind the bar. Further back, near the door to his office, what remained of the wheel-of-fortune still lay in pieces on the floor, smashed by booted feet.

Jean Claude came over from the faro table. He wore a greatcoat with a yellow muffler around his neck and he was carrying a carpetbag.

"Taking a trip?" asked Hobart, humorlessly.

"*Oui*. I have learned from past experience that sometimes a change of scenery is good for the health. I think I will visit my home in Baton Rouge. And then, who can say? Perhaps I will ply my trade on the riverboats once again."

"Yes. Eastern gentlemen are generally better losers."

"What of you, *M'sieu* Hobart? What are your plans?"

"You talk like it's finished here."

Jean Claude was startled. *"Je ne sais pas.* I do not know. But I have a feeling . . ."

Hobart nodded, suddenly exhausted. "Yes, I understand. A change of scenery."

"I am not alone in this. There are others who even now make their plans to depart. The eastbound train leaves at noon, or thereabouts. I will have many acquaintances with which to pass the time."

"Well. Good luck, then. Don't take any wooden nickels."

"Au revoir. A tout à l'heure."

"You never know."

Jean Claude passed on out. Hobart went to his office, deep in thought. He wondered if it wasn't time for him to seek greener pastures as well. *The rats,* he mused, *are deserting the sinking ship.* It was in the air. Little Texas had the feel now of a ghost town, abandoned and derelict, the ambience of a place where only spirits would dwell henceforth. The Texas Side had died. If not that, it was mortally wounded and waiting helplessly for the killing blow.

Engrossed in these observations, he was all the way into his office before he realized that the room was already occupied. A man with longish black hair, gray duster, and buckskin leggins was in his chair. At Hobart's entrance he lazily swung his legs off the desk. But he didn't go so far as to stand. For one brief, excruciating instant, Hobart thought that this man was a Texas trail hand, here with violence in mind. Then logic rescued him from panic. Obviously this one was no cowboy.

"Who are you?"

"The name's Reese. And you must be Mr. Hobart."

"That's right. Which explains why I'm here. Now why don't

you tell me what you're doing?"

"Didn't mean to startle you, Mr. Hobart."

It occurred to Hobart that Reese had to have slipped in by the back way; otherwise, surely, Jean Claude or the swamper would have issued warning.

"You didn't," he lied, poker-faced, and walked on over to the desk. Opening up the cigar box, he took out a long nine, thought it over, then pushed the box across to Reese.

Reese said, "Thanks." He ran the cigar under his nose, then held it up to his ear and rolled it between finger and thumb. "I seen somebody do this somewhere," he admitted boyishly.

"Looks like you know what you're doing."

"You have yourself a nice place here, Mr. Hobart."

Hobart sighed. "It has seen better days." The stove over in a corner had been stoked and the room was blessedly warm. He removed his gloves, stuffed them in a pocket of the overcoat, and then draped hat and coat on the rack. He settled into one of the deal chairs facing the desk. Taking a China match from a jade bowl on the desk, he scraped it to flame on his heel and lit the cigar clenched in his teeth, Reese watched every move he made. Then the gunslinger nodded at the grizzly pelt that covered most of the office floor.

"You bag that yourself, Mr. Hobart?"

"I don't kill things."

"I do."

Hobart nodded.

"But that ain't why I'm here," continued Reese, lighting up his own stogie, rolling the tip above the flame, as he had seen Hobart do, to get an even burn.

"I'm listening," was Hobart's equable reply.

"I know what's going on," said Reese. "I know the whole story. In fact, Tyler Kane brought me all the way up here to kill the gamblin' man. You know, your man Stanhouse."

"What makes you think he's mine?"

"Well." Reese shrugged. "He ran a table in your place. You

just went to the *juzgado* to have a visit with him. And people say you might try to get him out of lockup and onto a fast pony bound for nowhere."

"I see." Hobart blew smoke. "If he's my man, then why are you here telling me you were hired to kill him?"

"Not anymore. Tyler Kane welshed on the deal. He said my services were no longer required."

"This Tyler Kane. Any relation to one Murdoch Kane?"

"Thought you knew. Murdoch was Tyler's eldest boy. And the cowboy that Stanhouse killed was one of Tyler's hands."

"I did not have the occasion, two years ago, to meet Mr. Kane."

"You may yet get the chance."

"So what's your proposition, Mr. Reese?"

Reese leaned forward, planting his elbows wide on the desk, grinning like a wolf over the cigar.

"Would it be worth something to you if I could get Lee Stanhouse out of Two Rivers safe and sound?"

Hobart was silent a moment, deliberating on this unexpected offer and thinking about Stanhouse and what Stanhouse seemed to want.

"It might be," he replied, noncommital. "But Stanhouse doesn't want to be saved. He's ready to die."

Reese, shaking his head slowly, sat back in the desk chair.

"I can tell you this much for certain, Mr. Hobart. I have come across a number of *hombres* who thought they were ready to die. But when the time came, they had what you might call a change of heart."

Hobart made up his mind. "How much?"

"Well, how much is it worth to you?"

"I wouldn't pay you a plugged nickel for the gambler's life. But I'll give you a thousand dollars to steal the pleasure of killing him from this Tyler Kane and his wild drovers."

Reese studied the saloon owner for a moment. Hobart said it with such ardor that there was no doubting he had stated bona fide motives.

"They might turn around and take it out on you," remarked the gunslinger.

Hobart grunted. "Like I give a damn. How will you go about it?"

"Oh, I'll just convince that starpacker that it's in his best interests."

"So you plan to take on Clem Brackett?" Hobart was skeptical.

Reese was provoked by the other's doubt. "You don't think I can?"

"I don't know. I wouldn't make a wager either way. And if that's your plan I think I'll wait till it's done to pay you. I'm not in the habit of throwing my money away."

"*When* it's done I may not have the leisure to come strollin' back here to collect," protested Reese. "And you might not be around. If you know what I mean."

"That's a chance you'll have to take," said Hobart, unyielding. "You strike me as a man who likes to take an occasional chance."

Reese pursed his lips. "Half now. Then, when it's over, you can get the rest to me."

Hobart said, "Bottom right drawer. A strongbox. Take it out."

Reese opened the drawer, looked down, and then back at Hobart, surprised. He lifted the metal box and put it on the desk between them and considered the padlock.

"Feels heavy. Must be a lotta money."

Hobart tossed him the key. "Open it up. Take out five hundred."

Reese grinned. "You trust me? Why, I might get the notion to take it all."

"You might." Hobart's gaze was unflinching and as hard as tempered steel.

Reese made up his own mind then. "You've got guts," he said with admiration, then he unlocked and removed the padlock and opened the strongbox. Hobart watched him count out the greenbacks. Reese closed and secured the box and put it back into the bottom drawer.

"There," he said. "And I'll trust you for the balance. Partners ought to trust each other, right?"

The sound of horses came from Smoke Street. A lot of horses, at the gallop. Reese stood up quickly, by reflex squaring off at the door leading to the saloon proper. Hobart didn't move an inch.

"You better be quick about it, Reese," he suggested calmly. "That was justice, Texas-style, riding into town."

Chapter Twenty

Clem Brackett had just stepped out of the jail and was on his way to the town council meeting at McKaskle's general store when he saw the riders appear at the far end of Smoke, a thousand feet away.

The Texans spread out across the street and came charging hell-for-leather into the teeth of the wind, their longcoats flapping, quirts snapping, and horses snorting. It was a wild, grand sight, and Brackett stood at the edge of the boardwalk and admired it, with fear and exhilaration surging simultaneously through him. The thunder of pounding hooves rebounded off the drab false fronts of the Texas Side buildings. It occurred to Brackett that the most ominous aspect of this cowboy onslaught was the grim silence of the horsemen. Every other time Brackett had witnessed trail hands racing up or down Smoke they had been whooping it up. Not these men, though. Not this time. This was deadly serious business.

Brackett also had time to note that not another living soul was visible along Smoke—or Main, either. The people of Two Rivers, both north and south of the deadline, had felt the

Texans coming just as surely as they felt the approach of the winter storm.

They were halfway up Smoke before Brackett turned on his heel and stepped back inside the jail. He entered in time to see Patch back away from a gunport. Russell kept backing up until he fetched up against the desk. Then he looked at Brackett and Clem's spine crawled. Irish had been right. Patch had no stomach for facing trouble head-on. He had a streak of cowardice, and it was shining bright in his one good eye at this moment.

Brackett snarled, "The odds too long for you, Linus?"

Russell grunted. Brackett couldn't tell if the deputy was trying to say something with his ruined mouth or if it was just terror squeezing the air out of his lungs. But Patch's expression was loud and clear, a plea for deliverance.

"Here's your big chance," pressed Brackett, giving no quarter. "These men aren't the men who destroyed your farm and family, but they're cut from the same cloth. You'll never have a better excuse for retribution."

The riders were pulling up in front of the jail. Their horses pranced and blew. In crisis, all of Brackett's senses were heightened. He heard the whisper of metal on leather as rifles came out of saddle scabbards. The ratcheting of more than a dozen lever actions was loud in his ears, but he kept Russell pinned with a merciless glare. He had the sudden urge to take this backshooting coward by the collar and belt and pitch him out to the wolves. But he knew that he could never do it. Not out of concern for Russell but rather because, in his own way, he was as proud and stubborn as those Texas boys out there, and he was definitely determined now that they would not have their way. Not in his town.

"I'm going out there," he said tersely. "Bar the door behind me. Then take up that Davenport and put it out through the port. Break out the window glass. I want them to know that it's there. Do you understand?"

Patch nodded, trying to get a grip on himself.

"Just one more thing," added Brackett, fierce. "Don't be the one who fires the first shot. If you do, and if I live through what follows, so help me God I'll kill you with my bare hands."

The Winchester 44/40 in hand, Brackett pivoted and, bold as brass, stepped back out onto the boardwalk.

Russell wasted no time dropping the bar on the door. Brackett was confronted by seventeen hard and resolute men arrayed on their horses before him. There was no retreat available to him. An odd warmth rushed through his veins, casting back the icy chill of the morning. He was an eyelash away from death; he half expected a quick signal from Riley Davis—or the man he took to be Tyler Kane, the one with the ice-blue eyes that cut right through him—followed by a crashing fusillade of fatal gunfire. He braced himself for the swarm of lead that would take him down. He could visualize his bullet-torn carcass sprawled across the boardwalk, his blood leaking through the spaces between the weathered planks. And he thought, *there is something to be said for a son or daughter knowing that their father died standing up for what he believed in. It would have to be worse, knowing that he turned his back and walked away from trouble.*

But no signal was given, no deadly volley. The Texans looked upon this lone man with some measure of grudging regard, rifles ready in their gloved hands, their hard-run horses restless beneath them.

"You men are on the wrong side of the deadline," Brackett said, his voice rock-steady.

Lon Banks hawked and spat. "That's what we think of your deadline. Come on and try to arrest us."

Brackett fixed his attention on this one, knowing from experience that every mob had its firebrand and that sometimes you had to knock that man down one way or another.

"Hold it, Banks," rasped Kane.

"You know why we're here," Davis told Brackett. "We want the gambler. And we want the deputy that backshot my man. I don't have to tell you what..."

He was interrupted by the crash of breaking glass. Their nerves as taut as new-strung barbed wire, every Texan jerked in his saddle. Brackett tensed as some of the rifles swept down, and from the corner of his eye he saw the snout of Russell's scattergun protrude from one of the gunports on the right-hand window.

"Hold your fire!" barked Kane, throwing up a hand and trying to control his skittish bay.

"That's good advice," sounded Brackett.

Kane dragged his gaze from the menace of the shotgun and glowered at Brackett.

"What kind of man are you?" snarled the Triangle boss. "And what kind of law protects murderers from justice?"

"There are different brands of justice," Brackett replied. "But one kind of law, as far as I'm concerned."

"Trail-town law," snapped Kane, contemptuous.

"The kind that says a man gets a fair trial before justice takes his life."

"Who's behind that greener?" demanded Riley Davis.

"Who do you think?"

Kane gave Davis an I-told-you-so look. "There's a sample of his law. That murderous scum ought to be in a cage but instead it still wears a badge."

"Don't rile him too much," warned Brackett. "He has a powerful dislike for range riders, and that trigger is honed down."

Russell's unseen but very real presence had the effect on these men that Brackett had hoped for. He could see them judging the spread of a shotgun blast and the damage it could do to their close-up ranks at this range. And whether it was knowledge gleaned firsthand or second, they were all aware of what Patch Russell was capable of. Now they felt just as exposed as Brackett had felt stepping out onto the boardwalk to face them.

Kane was looking the jail over speculatively. What he saw was a fortress with foot-thick walls of brick and doors and shutters fashioned from weathered wood that was just this side of iron-hard. It would take shot and shell from a cannon to make a breach. Stymied in this way, his rage swelled into a barely containable firestorm.

"You goddamn tin star," he snarled furiously. "Give up those two men or you'll wish you'd never left your mother's womb."

The corner of Brackett's mouth curled up. He scanned the cluster of sun-darkened features and identified the two RD Connected men Davis had bailed out of lockup the morning before.

"I thought I told you two not to come back to town."

This caught them off guard. The two trail hands in question looked furtively at one another and then to Davis, who was regarding Brackett as he might a raving lunatic.

"Now just a damned minute . . . !" he blustered.

But Brackett, with fierce elation, saw his opening. He strode forward off the boardwalk, homing in on the two cowboys, watching them flirt with the idea of shooting him or running away or just standing fast. But Lon Banks, yanking savagely on rein leather and digging spurs deep, intervened by putting his horse athwart Brackett's path.

"Why not try me on for size, lawman?" Banks challenged.

Kane and the Triangle hands peered at Lon Banks with curious awe. This was not the same Lon Banks they had come to know. It was as though Grady Harmon's rash, dangerous spirit had possessed Lon, evicting the soft-spoken, good-natured, passive individual they had grown accustomed to.

Brackett looked up at Banks. He had no anger and no fear,

nothing but cold, detached logic telling him that he had to take this man down. He knew that if he tried to drag Lon from the saddle he would likely have the Winchester repeater Banks brandished going off in his face. So instead he grabbed the offside stirrup, lifting and shoving at the same time, putting everything he had into the effort. Lon let go of the rifle in order to get both hands under him to meet the hardpack. Lon's horse, wall-eyed, went up on its hind legs. Brackett uttered a raspy *"Hiya!"* and slapped the horse across the muzzle with his hat as the animal descended. The horse took off at a gallop from a standing start, colliding with some of the other mounts and causing a brief storm of chaotic action before breaking free of the bunch and taking off down Main with a violent combination of head jerks and back leg kicks that were reflexes from long ago but not forgotten bronco days.

Shaken, Lon rolled over on his back and saw Brackett closing in. With white-hot humiliation searing through him, a killing craze blinded him to the risks involved in going for the gun in his holster. All he saw was Brackett, and all he wanted to see were his bullets punching into the lawman's chest. He slapped his hand down on the butt of the Colt revolver, cursing as the hammer thong obstructed his draw. Then the gun was free. Brackett timed his kick perfectly, and the gun went spinning through a forest of horses' legs. Lon snarled something incoherent as the pain from a fractured middle finger lanced up his arm and into his shoulder. Brackett reached down and gathered him up with a handful of shirt and jacket—he still grasped the 44/40 in one hand. As he left the ground, Lon lashed out with his quirt. Brackett flinched at the sting of the rawhide slicing open his cheek, and it threw him off. Lon pursued his advantage with a wild punch that caught Brackett on the cheekbone just below the eye, grazing his nose. Brackett spun away, his eyes full of funny lights and his stomach doing a slow, sick roll. His legs got as rubbery as a foal's, and he went down. A cry of savage exultation bursting from his lips, Lon stepped in and kicked, aiming for Brackett's rib cage but striking the hipbone instead. Brackett rolled away. Encouraged, Banks kicked out once more. Brackett blunted the impact with a flailing arm. Quickly he brought his other arm around and hooked Lon behind the knees. Lon fell forward on top of him. Brackett punched the Triangle rider in the kidney even as he rolled out from under. He pushed to his feet. His hip protested with a peculiar hot numbness. He stumbled, yet managed to stay upright with a graceless shuffle-step. Vaguely aware of the tight circle of horsemen, he concentrated specifically on the heavy approach of his immediate adversary. He could feel Lon's attack vibrate through the hardpack and turned to meet it, taking Lon's shoulder in the breadbasket. All of the air was punched out of his lungs. He clamped an arm around the cowboy's neck, locking Lon's head against his side in a stranglehold. Driven backwards, Brackett focused on his feet, striving to keep from going down, and was propelled into a clumsy backwards run by Lon's driving impetus, only to collide with the crosspiece of the hitching post in front of the jail. The fresh pain this brought him was dulled significantly by the satisfaction he derived from feeling Lon's skull strike the post solidly. All the strength seemed to pour out of Banks. Brackett let him fall.

Heaving air, Brackett let the post support him for a few precious, revitalizing seconds. He raised the back of a hand to his cheek. It came away smeared thickly with dark blood. Then he gathered himself up and pushed away, quelling the pain that wracked his body, sighting his Winchester ten feet away in the dust and taking a step towards it.

He heard someone bark, "Now's our chance. Let's take him!" and with a fatalistic sigh he mentally checked for the weight of the Remington at his side and the Porterhouse under his arm even as he listened for the deadly percussion of Russell's greener.

"Stand clear, boys, or meet your Maker!"

Brackett surveyed the press of trail hands. His vision was blurred, as though he were submerged in a clear stream and looking up at them through its rippled surface. Their heads were turned away from him, and then they were pulling their horses back, separating into two groups, and Brackett remembered something about a Red Sea parting even as his gaze fell on Magruder. Daybreak was pushing the wheelchair across Main, for Magruder's hands were occupied with the long-barreled Dance revolvers he aimed democratically at the Texans.

"Back in my young days," remarked Magruder, as affably as if they were all chewing the breeze round campfire, "I was set upon by a passel of Crow one fine December morning, up around the Animas. The rascals helped themselves to all of my possibles, including my buckskins and buffalo coat. Left me out in the high country snow bare-ass naked. They thought it was a great joke to pull on a hair-face like me, and they figured I was a goner for sure. Ask me how cold it was. Well, I'll tell you. It was so cold I had icicles hanging out of my nose, so long I kept tripping over them. Why, it was so cold your breath would freeze up into a ball of ice, and you had to walk around it to keep from running smack into it and hurting yourself. Of course, those damned thieving Crow had purloined my Manton rifle and my Arkansas Toothpick and all my traps, so I couldn't even get me a pelt to cover myself with. I traipsed through those mountains for four days and nights before I happened up on Ike Sheltoe and his crew. And I came away from that without a touch of frostbite."

The Texans were exchanging bewildered glances by now. During his narrative Magruder had raised one of the revolvers briefly, and Daybreak had responded by halting their progress before they got in recklessly close to the riders.

Magruder said, "The point of that little anecdote is this. I am not that impervious to inclement weather conditions these days. I have squandered almost all of my youthful resilience. And while I may look as cozy as a flea on a fireside housecat under all these blankets, I am, if the truth be known, freezing my butt off. So if you don't mind, I'd be obliged if you'd make your choice with dispatch. All one of you boys has to do is start the shooting and we will commence with the fandango."

None of the Texans made a play. Not one wanted to be the instigator. They had the numbers in their favor, but they had been tactically outflanked, with Magruder on one side, Russell on the other, and Brackett in their midst. For his part, Brackett felt like laughing out loud. Magruder hadn't been prattling just to hear the sound of his own voice. That good-natured account had brought the tension down a few notches. Brackett discerned this much: in the back of their minds the drovers had reckoned on much less resistance. They had expected their tough reputation and the magnificent menace of their arrival to carry the day.

Like Brackett, Kane was reading his men. He saw that they had been intimidated, at least temporarily.

"Marshal," he said gravely, "this doesn't end it. We're not going to pack it up until we've done what we came here to do. I'll give you one hour to walk away and leave those murderers to us. After that, if you haven't backed off, it'll be too late for you *and* this town. We'll tear Two Rivers apart."

"Now, or an hour from now, you'll have to go through me, Kane."

Kane nodded. He had expected nothing less.

"It's your call." Kane turned in his saddle. "Two of you men get Lon across a saddle."

Brackett made no objection. As far as he could see, there was no purpose to be served in throwing the unconscious cowboy into a cell. His injuries stiffening up, he fetched his hat and Winchester while two of the Triangle boys dismounted to pick Lon up and drape him over one of their horses. The man whose saddle was occupied by the senseless Banks took up his reins, glanced at Kane for the go-ahead, and began trudging across Main toward Smoke Street. The rest of the riders, including Davis, began to filter away also. Kane hung back for the final word.

"One hour, Marshal," he reminded. "And then we'll settle our differences once and for all."

Brackett said nothing. They had passed the point of tough talk and brave posturing.

As Kane followed the rest of the horsemen, Magruder laid the Dance revolvers in his lap and rolled himself closer to Brackett. Daybreak followed, her eyes solicitous as they took in Brackett's gashed and swollen face.

"Well, so much for your good looks, Clem," declared Magruder. "You'll have a nice scar to remember this event by."

"Don't mean to sound ungrateful, Mac, but this isn't your fight. Stay out of it."

Magruder's abrupt laugh was humorless. "Can't do that. We got you into this, so it is incumbent upon us to try to get you out."

"Mac . . ."

"God in heaven, man!" gruffed Magruder, exasperated. "You can rant and rave all you want . . . *after* we get inside."

Brackett had no further argument. He got Magruder up onto the boardwalk with Daybreak's assistance, then laid his fist against the door several times.

"Russell! Open up!"

The crossbar was lifted, the door opened, and Lee Stanhouse stood there with his soft and sardonic smile.

"I hate to be the bearer of bad tidings, Marshal, but your deputy has deserted the cause. He paused in his decampment only long enough to unlock the door to my cell and advise me to make a run for it myself."

A curse on his lips, Brackett brushed past the gambler. Once inside he looked to the window where all along he had believed

Russell to be. The sawed-off Davenport had been wedged fast into the gunport. Magruder and Daybreak entered behind him and Stanhouse shut the door.

"Why didn't you light out?" asked Magruder.

"Because," Stanhouse reminded them, "I am the guest of honor."

Chapter Twenty-One

All the way out to the Brackett house, Irish Joe Kempen was tormented by indecision. Every step closer brought a new resolve to turn back. But the resolve would crumble like worm-eaten wood before the vision of Maris. He argued with himself that there was nothing wrong in bidding her farewell. That in fact it would be remiss of him not to do so. After all, on numerous occasions he had come to dinner with Clem and his wife, and he and Maris had become friends. And then he would counter this argument with another, for he alone was privy to his real motivation. His feelings for Maris exceeded the boundary of friendship. He had lain awake long into the night tortured by fantasies that centered around her. This was his secret shame, and he would curse himself for imagining what might have been if she and his best friend had not married, and worse, what would happen if Brackett were gone from the scene.

His ticket for passage on the Overland was in his pocket. His warbag was slung on his shoulder and his stick was tied to his belt. He did not wear gun and shellbelt—these were stashed in the warbag. He had cut across the open fields of straw-colored grass from his boarding house on Willow toward the Kearney road, avoiding the streets and the risk of meeting townspeople. He assumed that the word was already out. About how he had quit on Brackett at a time when his friend needed him most. The most frustrating thing about it all was that he knew he was both right and wrong. He had reached the conclusion that sometimes, in certain situations, concepts of right and wrong just could not be applied. And all that was left for a man to do was what had to be done.

Striding moodily through the high grass toward the scattering of houses on the eastern outskirts of town, he felt the first spray of rain driven by the wind. He cast a look behind him. Wisps of cloud drifted like gunsmoke over the rooftops of Two Rivers, so low that it draped the top floor of The Plainsman. A gray, bleak, miserable day—quite suited to Kempen's frame of mind. At one point he thought he heard the thunder of many horses on the run, but he looked in the direction of town and saw nothing move but trash blowing in the alleys. The wind howled like a banshee in his ears and he moved on.

A few paces short of the Brackett house he hesitated and found himself throwing furtive looks this way and that. His approach had brought him to the back of the house, and he toyed with the idea of going around to come in by the road. He told himself that this was foolishness, and climbed up into the dogtrot, his heels clomping hollowly on the planking.

The door to the bedroom opened quickly. Maris emerged, and as usual her golden beauty struck him like a blow to the midsection, shortening his breath. He watched a rapid play of emotions on her winsome, windswept features: hope dashed into deep disappointment followed by a flash of restrained terror. *She was hoping it was Clem*, realized Irish. *Brackett, you're the complete and utter fool. And the luckiest man alive.*

Irish held up a hand, "It's not what you think, Maris. Nothing's happened to Clem. I've just come to . . . to say so long."

"So long?" Maris looked at the warbag. "You're leaving." It was an observation, not a question.

Kempen nodded and looked away from her eyes. In so doing

his restless gaze fell upon the trunk and valise on the floor of the bedroom behind her.

"My God, Maris," he breathed, aghast. "What are you doing?"

She shut the door.

"Come into the kitchen," she urged. "I've got coffee on the stove."

Crossing the dogtrot, she preceded him into a room that was cozy warm and redolent with the aroma of java. Using a potholder, she carried the enameled coffeepot to the counter and poured the Arbuckle into two pewter cups. Irish set his warbag down by the door. As he sat down his stick banged against the chair, so he untied it from his belt and propped it against the wall. Leaning forward he clasped his big rough hands together on the table and stole a glance at her. She had her back to him, and he sensed that she was reluctant to turn around. She was wearing a pretty blue dress adorned with the print of tiny white flowers. He couldn't help but admire the slim taper of her waist, the firm round curve of her hips. Her golden hair was done up, and he appreciated the sweet and graceful lines of her neck and the way soft, undone tendrils caressed it. He wondered how any man could honestly believe that there was anything in life more important than a priceless woman like this.

"So you're leaving, too," he muttered.

"I thought about it," she confessed, contritely. "My father lives in Broken Bow. I thought about going to see him. I had everything packed. And then I sat down to rest. I shouldn't have done *that*. Idle hands breed idle thoughts, don't they? I started to think about what I was doing. I guess I must have sat there for an hour. Thinking. And I . . . I decided I *couldn't* leave."

Kempen's wildest hope died stillborn. Something twisted up inside him and then abruptly smoothed itself out as she turned to carry the cups of coffee to the table. His attention was drawn to the bulge of her belly. *You bastard,* he chided himself with acrid self-disgust. He had forgotten about the child. Clem's child. She put the cup before him and sat down across from him. He smiled sadly at her and she smiled back, a wise and understanding and in a way apologetic smile.

"Do you know what happened last night?" he asked.

"Eli Kesserling came by to tell me that Clem was safe. It was very late. Clem had brought his horse over to the livery. He didn't want to leave it out in the weather all night. He was in a hurry to get back. At first I was upset that he was so close and yet didn't bother to come and see me. If only to tell me himself that he was all right, and not to worry. But then I realized that I had no right to expect that of him after what I had said and done. Eli asked him what had happened; I suppose everyone in town knew there had been gunplay down on the Texas Side. But Clem just told him that there had been a little trouble in Hobart's place and that it was over." She searched Kempen's face. "But it's not over, is it, Joe?"

"I don't know," said Irish. "But I guess it's over for me."

"Why?"

"Patch Russell murdered a trail hand, Maris. I saw him shoot the man down in cold blood. I tried to warn Clem. I told him it would happen. I'll have no part of it."

Maris sipped her coffee. Irish watched her and dreamed how wonderful it would be to sit down to coffee every morning with her. Ruthlessly, he crushed the notion.

"Where will you go?" she asked.

Irish shrugged. No place far from Maris held any allure. "The goldfields. Maybe Santa Fe to get a job with a freighting outfit. I don't know."

"We'll miss you."

We. The word echoed brutally in Kempen's ears. With that one word Maris had shown him where she stood. His cheeks were hot with shame. She knew why he had really come. He could try to fool himself, but he couldn't fool her. Women had a keen and faultless instinct when it came to affairs of the heart.

He stood up suddenly, his coffee untouched. He stared down at her, trying to etch her face into his memory, and he wondered if that memory would serve to warm him in the cold and lonesome nights to come or merely add to his suffering.

"I'd better get going," he said gruffly. "I just came by to . . ." He cut it short. There was no point in lying to her. She knew his reasons. So he turned and slung the warbag over his shoulder and opened the door. The bitter wind greeted him. A gust of driven rain slashed against the kitchen window. Thunder rolled across the plains and shook the earth.

"Joe . . ."

He was too ashamed to look back. "Goodbye, Maris," he said, choking on the words, and fled the room.

Hearing his rapid departure on the dogtrot, Maris whispered, "Clem needs you, Joe. He needs both of us. And we both need him."

More footsteps, quick and hard. Maris looked with renewed hope at the door, a welcoming smile ready on her lips. It had to be Irish. A change of heart had turned him back. Everything would work out. And then the door opened and Irish stood there with a peculiar look on his face. He no longer carried the warbag. A man Maris had never seen appeared behind Kempen, a man in a long gray duster, with lank black hair and coyote eyes. The way he grinned at her fired a bolt of apprehension through Maris.

"Well," said Irish grimly, "I didn't get very far."

He stepped in and to one side, and Maris saw the gun in the stranger's hand.

"You Brackett's wife?"

Maris lifted her chin slightly. "I most certainly am."

Irish had half turned to face Reese. He, too, was looking at the pistol. Reese saw that, and read Kempen's mind.

"Come on," he goaded. "Show the little lady how brave you are. Don't think about it too long, though. You'll talk yourself out of it."

"Don't try it, Joe," pleaded Maris, afraid that Irish, in his present state of mind, would do something just that rash. "Please. Don't."

Irish glanced darkly at her, then uncoiled his muscles. With an ugly expression of contempt, Reese stepped in and straight-armed Irish in the chest. Kempen stumbled backward against the wall next to the kitchen table.

"What do you want?" snapped Maris.

"A trade," replied Reese. "You for the gambler that your husband is protecting." To Irish, he added, "You go give him my terms. I want to see that cardsharp walking up the road alone. Anybody else and Brackett might have to find himself another woman."

"Bastard," growled Kempen.

"Don't try to rile me. This is business. Get going."

Irish looked once more at Maris. He could not bring himself to leave her alone with this man.

"Don't worry about me," she said. "I'll be all right. Go on." She wanted Irish to leave. For his sake. She knew there was a strong chance he might try a stupid play that would wind up killing him. "Go get Clem," she persisted. "He'll do the right thing. He always does."

But Irish had closed his ears to her persuasion. Out of the corner of his eye he had seen the stick leaning against the wall, hard by the table leg, and within his reach. He had left it on his way out a few moments ago. It had been a part of the life he had thought to leave behind. He offered Maris an apologetic smile, resting his left hand on the back of the chair in which he had been sitting a while earlier.

"Yes," he said. "I reckon he will. And it's high time I did, too."

His grip tightened on the back of the chair. Mustering all the brawny strength housed in arm and shoulder, he hurled it straight into Reese, and in a smooth continuation of that fluid motion he turned his body and reached around with his right hand to grasp the stick.

A snarl of rage escaped Reese as he flung the chair aside. Irish rushed him, swinging the stick. Reese brought the gun back into line. Maris screamed, "No!" Kempen's aim was true, striking the gun solidly and driving it out of the pistolman's grasp. Irish threw his body into Reese and yelled, "Maris, run!" His charge carried Reese backward and cleared a path to the doorway for her. In a deadly embrace they slammed into the cannonball stove. Reese let out a howl as hot iron seared the backs of his legs. Maris leaped toward the door. Irish tried to raise the stick for another blow, but Reese grabbed it with his right hand, and drew his other pistol with the left. Grinning into Kempen's face, he put the barrel against Irish Joe's slab-hard belly and squeezed the trigger. The report was muffled. Maris had just made the dogtrot. The gunshot stopped her in her tracks. Horrified, she turned, and her hands flew to her lips as she tried to stifle the cry that welled up from her soul. Doubled over, Irish took two rigid steps back. The stick clattered to the floor. Reese shoved him savagely out onto the dogtrot. Irish staggered sideways and fell, curling. Maris slipped to her knees beside him but did not touch him, afraid that even the most gentle touch would only aggravate the unbearable agony that spasmed through Kempen.

Reese snatched her up by the hair and gave a painful wrench. She flailed at him with her fists. Reese spun her around and drove her face first into the most convenient wall. The impact triggered such excruciating pain in her swollen belly that Maris almost lost consciousness. Never in her life had she felt such pain. Crumpling, she uttered such an awful, guttural, wailing moan that even Reese was taken aback, his spine crawling. This was the horrible lament of a tormented animal, not the cry of a human being, and it momentarily shook the gunslinger to the core.

Gritting his teeth, Reese holstered his gun and used both

hands to drag Irish along the dogtrot to the front porch. He blinked against the rain whipping at him from every direction. Getting Kempen to the top of the steps, he straightened, put a boot to Irish's back, and shoved. Kempen flopped down the steps to land on his back in the yellow mud. Reese looked up and down the empty, storm-dark road, drew the Smith & Wesson once again, thumbed back the hammer and casually aimed at Kempen's head.

But the woman's cry would not stop ringing in his head. He couldn't silence it. The sound had torn through all the dark and vicious passion that fueled his hate and had touched the carcass of his conscience with the spark of life. Without understanding it fully, Reese found himself at the limit of his capacity for cruelty. That was a limit no man could exceed.

He raised the gun and fired two rounds into the gray, tempestuous sky. Holstering and turning, he went to Maris and carried her into the kitchen.

The gunshots disrupted Miss Pierce's reading lesson in the schoolhouse a quarter mile east along the Kearney road. The children left their desks and their *McGuffey's Readers* and stampeded for the westside windows, heedless of the schoolmarm's dire reprimands. Davey Lake was the first to see the body in front of the Brackett house. With a strangled cry he was out the door before Miss Pierce could even utter protest.

Irish was crawling out into the middle of the road when Davey reached him, sliding to his knees in the muck. Kempen felt the pressure of the boy's hands on his back and with all the strength and will left to him, rolled over. His arms were locked against his belly, and he drew his knees up and closed his eyes against the cold sting of the rain.

"Get . . . Brackett . . ."

Davey shot a quick glance at the house. Reese stepped out into the gloom of the dogtrot. At the same time he stepped out of Davey Lake's penny-dreadful fantasies and into harsh and frightening reality, for he had Maris clasped in front of him, an arm around her waist and a gun to her head. The way Maris looked scared Davey more than anything.

"Go get the marshal, boy," yelled Reese over the hiss of the rain and the wailing of the wind. "Tell him to send the gambler to me and he gets his wife back alive."

Then Davey was off and running once more, down the miring road into Two Rivers.

Chapter Twenty-Two

Banjo brewed up some coffee and they shook out their slickers and got them on when the rain started. Hunching down in the half-dry lee of the chuckwagon they drank their fast-cooling crank and hardly spoke to one another, lost in solitary and solemn introspection. Each of them considered a world turned on its end and hard-shaken; each, in his own way, tried to sift through the ruins.

An hour after Tyler Kane had ridden out of camp with Davis and the others, bound for Two Rivers and revenge, Carson poured the grounds out of his cup, stood up, laid the cup on the toolbox and looked down at Banjo and Yuby. He still had the Henry repeater in his grasp.

"I'm going in," he said with calm resolve. "What they're doing is wrong. They've got to be stopped."

Neither one of the others said anything to that.

"We're as much to blame as anyone else," continued Carson firmly. "We knew my father was wrong to hire that gunslinger. And even beyond that, he was wrong to want vengeance. It would've been different if that gambler had shot Murdoch for no reason. But it was self-defense, just like it was with Grady, and we all know it. Sure, Stanhouse is a cheat. But that is just not a good enough reason for killing. Truth is, we didn't any of us have the guts to stand up to my father and say no. It might be too late, but I for one have got to try."

"They're not after just the gambler," reminded Yuby. "They've gone for the one-eyed deputy, too. You and I both know that *was* murder, Carson."

"Maybe back in the old days you *had* to take the law into your own hands," replied Carson. "But times change. Now we've got real law out here, or at least the makings of it, and if it's going to work the way we want it to then we have to give it a chance. Only when it tries and fails should we take it on ourselves to see justice done."

Yuby stood up. "You went into The Palace last night with your mind set on killing that gambler."

Carson made a sharp, impatient gesture. "Hell, Yuby. I was as confused as my father. I was ashamed of him for hiring scum like Reese to do his dirty work for him. I wanted to show him up. And I guess I wanted to do something that would make him proud of me. I wanted to prove to him that I was a man who had what it took to live by the code he had lived by all his life. But I couldn't go through with it. You were there. You saw I couldn't do it. Sure, I had it all squared away in my head, but my heart wasn't in it. That code of honor is a good thing, sure. Until a man uses it to justify his own wrongdoing."

Banjo spoke up. "Men like Tyler will always live by it, all the same. They don't know any better. Don't want to." Chewing on the tip of his cold corncob pipe, he peered up at Carson from under the rain-heavy brim of his wideawake hat. "Tyler's done many a wrong thing in his life, especially of late. He sure hasn't done right by you, Carson. Not in my book, anyroad. But you're talking about going up against your own father with a gun in your hand."

"You might be walking into a bad spot," agreed Yuby. "One where you'll have to decide whether to use your gun on Tyler. Are you prepared to do that?"

Carson drew a deep and shaky breath. "I don't know."

"Don't put yourself in that position unless you're dead sure."

"I'm going into town," grated Carson stubbornly, spacing the words. "What are you going to do, Yuby? Try to stop me?"

Wellman smiled faintly. "No, sir. I'll be riding along with you. Before I was old enough to shave I had bought into enough trouble for a lifetime. When I got my discharge from the cavalry I promised myself that I would fight no more wars for anybody else. I'd mind my own business and not interfere in anyone else's. All I asked was that other folk show me the same courtesy. Problem is, sometimes other people don't abide by your own rules. They get bound and determined to lasso you into their business. Like they just can't handle all the trouble by themselves and they lay some of it off on you. I've about decided that the only thing worse than being on the wrong side of an issue is to stand in the middle. You tend to get caught in the crossfire. The Lord God Almighty put us all in the same stew together, and a man can't just up and decide he won't be one of the ingredients."

"Thanks, Yuby," said Carson, grateful.

"Don't thank me yet. I don't do things by halves. Particularly in this kind of work. I don't ride into trouble wondering if I can pull the trigger. Somebody draws on me and I'll do my level best to kill him first. And it won't make me no never mind who it is."

"I understand."

"Do you?" Yuby's voice was harsh. "Let me be sure. If your pa aims a gun at me I'll shoot him. I won't dally to find out if he really means it. And then, if you feel obliged to start a blood feud with me, I'll kill you, too, and be done with it."

Carson felt his nape hairs move, for when he searched Yuby's cold and fierce demeanor he saw that Wellman meant every word.

"This is the thing," explained Yuby. "I have seen men take the law into their own hands. All the bitterness that life breeds inside them is cut loose and takes over. They'll do things in the heat of the moment that you'd never in a million years expect them to do. You have to set yourself and be ready for that."

It was evident that Yuby carried the memory of a deep and very personal tragedy. But Carson didn't pry, he simply nodded, accepting Wellman's conditions, and turned to Stubbins, who was still hunkered morosely on the dry side of the Studebaker.

"What about it, Banjo? Will you come with us?"

Banjo shook his head sadly. "Reckon not, boy. Sorry. I've rode with your pa for almost twice as many years as you've got under your belt. He can be the most orneriest cuss, and he has made his share of mistakes, and nobody is more qualified to testify to that than yours truly. But it just ain't in me to go up against him the way you want to. I have given Tyler thirty years and then some. I gave him the sweat of my brow and the blood in my veins and every waking moment of my life. Even gave him a part of myself, that day we run down those Mex horse rustlers at Falfurrias." He held up his right hand. Carson knew the story of how Banjo had come to lose that thumb. It had been sheared clean off by a bullet during that shootout in Falfurrias, the summer before Carson had come squawling into the world. In this way Stubbins had earned his nickname: a banjo had four strings and Stubbins had four fingers left on that hand.

"Hell," continued Banjo, with a raspy laugh. "I can't even handle a sidegun anymore with my right, and I never could hit the side of a barn from inside with my left. I wouldn't be no good to you. And Yuby's all the way right. Your pa has been pushed too far this time. Sure, it's mostly his own damn fault. It looks like everything he had worked for all his life ain't worth a bucket of warm spit, after all. And he has lost both of his sons. That's the way he sees it. All he has left is his pride and the code that, in his day, men lived by and died for." Stubbins shook his head. "Don't care to see the two of you gunning each other, thanks all the same. I'll just sit this one out."

Carson went over and laid a hand on Banjo's bony shoulder. It was a gesture that needed no words. Then, with a curt nod to Yuby he sloshed across the camp toward the two horses, tethered beneath the wind-thrashed cottonwoods.

When Davey Lake came slogging down Main to the jail, Brackett was slumped in his desk chair, wincing as Daybreak dabbed at his slashed cheek with a whiskey-soaked rag. Clem had rejected her suggestion that she try for McKaskle's store, where medicine might be had. Brackett did not care for the idea of her braving streets that, for the moment, belonged to the Texans. It was at this point that Magruder had brandished the flask of Overholt from beneath his blanket. Stanhouse had pulled the extra chair over to the side of the desk and was playing a desultory game of solitaire. Clem had seen no point in locking him up again. The gambler apparently had no intention of making a break for parts unknown. Magruder watched his daughter's tender, loving ministrations with a bittersweet smile.

The tattoo of running feet on the boardwalk brought Brackett out of his chair with the violence of a bull firing out a chute. Magruder was reminded of the moment in his study two nights ago when distant gunfire had triggered the same reaction in his good friend. As he turned the wheelchair to face the door, Magruder regretfully gave his head a shake. Some men were picked by God, he reflected, to live out their lives on the cutting edge. He picked up the brace of Dance revolvers that had been resting on his wasted legs.

Davey beat his little fists wearily against the beams of the door and cried out Brackett's name. Clem surged forward, threw aside the bar and caught the boy as he half fell, exhausted, over the threshold.

"Somebody fetch a blanket," he rasped, kneeling, the youngster in his arms.

"Allow me," said Stanhouse, and rose to enter the cellblock, returning a moment later to find that Brackett had lifted Davey to a seat on the corner of the desk. The gambler draped the blanket over the youngster's shuddering shoulders. Magruder rolled himself over to shut and bar the door.

"Catch your breath, Davey," Brackett advised.

Davey gasped and gulped for a moment. He had a tight grip on Brackett's sleeve and a shocked glaze on his mud-splattered face. His stomach knotting into a cold fist, Brackett could tell that the boy had been a witness to something he was too young to handle.

"Your place..." panted Davey. "A man... a man shot Mr. Kempen... he... had a hold of Mrs. Brackett... he ...he said he'd trade her for... for... the gambler..."

Brackett slowly pried the boy's fingers from his sleeve and straightened.

"This man, can you describe him?"

Davey heaved in more air and steadied himself.

"He had hair like an Indian's. And... and he wore leggins."

"Who is it, Clem?" asked Magruder.

Brackett's voice was dead hollow. "Kane's gunslinger."

"Reese," muttered Magruder. "His name is Reese. Sigel mentioned it."

Brackett turned to Stanhouse. The gambler had shed that sardonic half-smile.

"Let me go, Marshal. He'll release your wife once he has me."

"He came here to kill you."

"I know that."

Brackett glanced at Davey, painfully aware that the boy was watching his every move and hanging on his every word. Something had gone terribly wrong, and Davey expected Brackett to put it right. Brackett realized then that there was a high price to the privilege of being the boy's idol. Beyond the obligations of his job and his duty to the law he had sworn to uphold, he was accountable to Davey Lake, for his actions now could in some measure be instrumental in the making of a man. The tin star was merely a symbol of his own personal pride;

Brackett had come to accept that in recent days. But for Davey he would have sacrificed that pride—he would have traded Stanhouse for Maris and walked away from Two Rivers and worried later about living with himself.

Stanhouse said, "You don't really have a choice, Marshal. Your hour of grace is almost past. Those Texans will be coming back soon, and this time they can't afford to let themselves be put off. And you can't be in two places at the same time. Let me go. Then you'll have your wife back safe and those cowboys will leave this town and its people be, and nobody will have to die."

"Except you."

"This is all my doing. A long time ago an innocent life was snuffed out on my account. I don't want that to happen again. Self-pity is a very selfish indulgence."

"God knows I wish I could," whispered Brackett in quiet agony.

"If I hadn't cheated Kane's son, none of this would have happened."

"What's done is done. Mac, take Daybreak and the boy out of here."

"I think I'll stay and keep an eye on things until you get back," said Magruder.

"I'm not going anywhere."

"The hell you aren't."

"I can't ask you to do this."

"I'm not asking you to ask me. And I'm not leaving. Unless you prove yourself tough enough to throw me out."

"Why are you doing this?"

"Let's just say that every man has to do his part for law and order. Now go on and take care of your wife, and kill that sonuvabitch while you're at it. Excuse the language, Davey. What's the matter with you, Clem? You think you can hold those Texas yahoos off single-handed, but you don't think I can, is that it? Well, that's always been your problem. You short-changed Irish and now you're doing me the same way."

Brackett couldn't figure out why Magruder was so determined to put himself between a rock and a hard place, but it was plain enough that he would not be swayed. And the thought occurred to Brackett that, this way, there was at least a chance for all of them, most of all Maris. A slim chance, but slim was better than none."

"Okay," he said. "On one condition. You've got to get your daughter and Davey out. Now. Before Kane and the others come back."

"You leave that to me. Now get going."

Brackett took up his Winchester, thought twice, and laid the repeater across the arms of Magruder's wheelchair.

"I'll have to get in close," he said. "So I won't be needing this. Not as badly as you might. And Mac, don't get yourself killed."

Magruder smiled. "Same to you."

"I'll slip out the back way. Daybreak, come bar the door behind me."

She followed him down the cellblock hall. He got the door open and took a careful look out, but before he could steal into the rain-swept alley she threw her arms around his neck and pressed her firm, desirable body against his. He felt her hot, sweet breath on his face, and then her lips brushed his before he could reach up and break her hold. Pushing her back to arm's length, he saw the tears welling in her smoky eyes.

"I love you, Clem Brackett." Her voice was husky and anguished.

"Don't say that!"

"I love you."

"Then I'm sorry," he muttered, miserably. "Because I love Maris. I'll die for her, gladly, if that's what it takes. More than that, I'd give up my star, my pride, everything for her. I know that now. Now that it might be too late. That's how much I love her, Daybreak. I know the way you feel. Don't you think I've seen the way you look at me? I should have come out and said all this a long time ago. But I . . . I kept putting it off. I suppose was hoping that your feelings would change. Because I didn't want to hurt you."

"Don't die for her. Come back to me."

"*Daybreak!*" It was Magruder, at the other end of the hall. "Let him go, child."

"I'll come back," Brackett promised. "But not for you. I'm sorry."

And then he was gone and she shut the door, but neglected to lift the bar into place. Turning to confront her father, she slacked against the strap-iron of a cell, as though drained of strength and will.

Magruder said, gently, "I warned you, girl. I had hoped to spare you. A poet by the name of Marvell put it very well. 'For Fate with jealous eyes does see Two perfect loves, nor lets them close: Their union would her ruin be, and her tyrannic power depose. And therefore her decrees of steel Us as the distant poled have placed.'" His tone was desolate. "Bar the door, Daybreak."

A lamp burned low on the wall just inside the doorway framing him. It did not dispel the gloom in which she stood at the far end of the cellblock, but it glimmered in her eyes as she raised her head slowly, and Magruder thought with a shudder. *Those are Arapaho eyes, as untamed and dangerous as a dog soldier's.*

Spinning, Daybreak threw open the door and was gone before he could call out.

"Daughter! No!" he groaned, not loudly, and thrust himself through the doorway adjoining office and cellblock. The stock of the Winchester caught the frame and the rifle looped off the arms of the wheelchair and clattered to the floor. He paid it no heed, hastening to the rear door. Once there he could go no further. It was one long step down into the muck of the alley. For him, it might have been a mile. The wild wind raged against him and kicked the door shut in his face. He leaned forward, pushing with both hands, and threw the door open once more, but the wind did not relent, and as he cried his daughter's name it slammed the door against him a second time.

"A woman once loved me like that."

Magruder turned the wheelchair. Stanhouse stood in the office doorway. He held the Winchester. Not exactly aiming it but close enough to make Magruder wonder.

"It doesn't pay to love so completely," the gambler went on. "The heart is too fragile. You can't leave it unprotected."

"If she loved him, she'd let him go."

Stanhouse raised a brow. "You think so?"

"What are you going to do?" growled Magruder, though he already knew.

"Why, I'm going to do my part. This is what you said every man should do, remember?"

"And if I try to stop you. You'll shoot?"

"We won't have to find out," replied Stanhouse with mild reproof. "Because you won't try."

Chapter Twenty-Three

Brackett found Irish lying in the road, curled up in a tight ball, covered with cold yellow mud. Bending down, he pressed his fingers against the side of Kempen's neck, and holding his breath, searched for a pulse. It was weak and erratic, but it was there, and Brackett thanked a merciful God for that.

Hearing a door open, he straightened as Reese appeared in the dogtrot. The gunslinger was using Maris as a shield, with one arm clamped tightly around her waist, the barrel of his gun pressed against the side of her head. Maris had her arms clasped to her belly and there was not a trace of color in her face. The poison of a murderous rage swept through Brackett so strongly that he began to shake. He had killed men before. Always in self-defense, always in the heat of the moment, with no other recourse and with at least some remorse coming later. But this was different. This time it would be a pleasure.

"Well, Marshal," drawled Reese. "I think you've made a mistake."

"No. You have."

He began walking toward the house.

"I guess he don't care what happens to you, little lady," Reese murmured in Maris's ear.

She watched Brackett coming on. All the light had gone from

her eyes, and all the life out of her expression.

Reaching the steps of the porch, Brackett said, sneering, "That's your style, Reese. Hiding behind a woman. You gunslingers are all the same. Big talk, no guts."

"All you had to do was cut the gambler loose," complained Reese. "It didn't have to come to this."

"You and Kane," rasped Brackett, contemptuous. "Cut from the same yellow cloth, aren't you? He hires the likes of you to do his killing for him. And you hide behind a woman and shoot down an unarmed man."

"Let's get this straight. I don't work for Tyler Kane no more. And I'm not here to kill the gambler. I work for Hobart now, you fool. He hired me to get Stanhouse out of your jail and out of this town. I got two horses tied up out back. See for yourself, if you don't believe me."

"*You* get it straight," said Brackett fiercely, climbing up onto the porch. "This is between you and me now. This has nothing to do with Stanhouse or Kane or Hobart. Not anymore. That's my friend out there bleeding in the road, and that's my wife you've got under the gun."

"*That's far enough!*" yelled Reese as he sidestepped across the dogtrot, putting his back to the kitchen door. "I'll kill her. Don't think I won't."

"Then I'll send you straight to hell."

"What kind of man are you?" grated Reese feverishly. "You're so proud you'd let her die just to get to me!"

"He's the best and bravest man I've ever known," said Maris huskily, staring into Brackett's eyes.

"*Shut up!*" shouted Reese, shaking her so viciously that a low moan escaped her bloodless lips. She sagged in the gunman's grip as fresh pain shot through her.

"Let her go, you bastard," whispered Brackett, trembling.

"I will. As soon as you get rid of your guns. I don't want to have to kill you, Marshal. That's not what I'm getting paid for. That man out there, he came at me. I was defending myself. I'll defend myself against you if need be. But I've got no quarrel with you."

"Yes you do."

"Lay 'em down," warned Reese. His tone had an ugly ring of finality.

Brackett gave Maris one more long look. Then he reached around with his left hand, using thumb and forefinger to bring the Remington out of his side holster.

"Toss it out in the road," Reese ordered.

Brackett did so.

"And the other one. I know you carry a second under your coat."

Brackett slowly removed the Porterhouse and hurled it away. It smacked into the mud at the foot of the porch steps.

Reese relaxed a notch, now that he held the upper hand once more.

"Let her go," repeated Brackett.

"I knew you were a reasonable man. So am I. Now we're all going to step inside. You're gonna sit down in there, and that's where you'll stay until I ride out. And don't come after me, lawman. Don't come after me and I won't come back this way again. Ain't that reasonable?"

"Sounds reasonable," agreed Brackett flatly.

Reese kicked the door open and backed into the kitchen. Brackett followed. The gunslinger stepped backward to the counter, half-carrying Maris, and Brackett shut the door, making no sudden moves. Reese gave Maris a shove that propelled her, stumbling, into Brackett's arms. Brackett pressed her tight against him. She laid her head on his shoulder, shivering, but her eyes were dry. Brackett felt pride and love swelling in his chest.

"Well," said Reese, "I reckon I'll be going." He pursed his lips, thinking something over, then reached under his shirt and placed the roll of greenbacks he extracted onto the counter.

"If you see Hobart, Marshal, you can give him back this money. Business is business, right? I've got my reputation to think of. Hell, I'm not greedy. Tyler Kane paid me for my time. The trip wasn't a total loss. Now, why don't you two stand away from that door?"

Brackett stepped to one side, turning Maris to place himself between her and the gunslinger. Reese circled the room with the wariness of a cornered animal, past the counter and the rain-splashed window, past the stove, sidestepping, his Smith & Wesson all the time aimed at the marshal. Brackett watched the man's coyote eyes, ignoring the gun. When he saw those eyes flick to the door to guide a groping hand to the latch, Clem slipped his own hand into the pocket of his coat.

"Reese," he whispered, breaking free of Maris and stepping into the middle of the kitchen, well away from her.

Reese jerked his head around.

Brackett said, "You're not going anywhere."

He drew Stanhouse's Sharps derringer and fired.

Reese was slammed back against the door, grunting as the bullet struck him high in the center of the chest. He stared at the smoking hideout in Brackett's hand like he was trying to figure out what it was. Then he lurched forward, convulsed, tottered on his toes, and coughed up a dark smattering of blood. He raised his head to give Brackett a bloody grin as he strained to lift his gun.

Maris screamed, "No!" and launched herself at Brackett, throwing herself into the line of fire. Brackett desperately spun her around. The door flew open behind Reese, but the pistolman didn't have time to turn. Brackett braced himself for the impact of hot lead as gunshots rang out, filling the kitchen with deadly thunder, and he watched the gunslinger's chest open up with an appalling explosion of blood and bone fragments, even as one of the bullets passing through Reese whined dangerously close, to smack into the wall behind him.

Reese fell, revealing Daybreak standing in the doorway beyond, soaked to the skin and splattered with mud. Brackett's Remington was still smoking in her hands.

He left Maris leaning weakly against the counter. Stepping over the body, he went to Daybreak and gently pried the gun from her grasp, looking into those dark and savage eyes, searching for words. Before he could find the right ones, Maris cried out in wrenching pain. Brackett spun to see her slide to the floor, clutching her swollen belly. With a strangled cry of his own, he rushed to her, thinking for one horrible instant that she had been shot.

"I'm all right," Maris gasped, quick to lessen his agony.

Daybreak knelt down on the other side of her.

"I will stay with her," she told Brackett.

Maris put a hand on his chest, felt the rapid pounding of his strong heart, and smiled the best she could.

"Go on, Clem. If you've still got work to do, then go on. I'll be fine. And I'll be waiting for you. I'll be right here when you finish."

Daybreak measured the depth of feeling that poured out of Brackett as he gazed at Maris, and even as her heart twisted, a pure and selfless warmth invaded her. Much to her astonishment, she found that she could take comfort in Brackett's happiness even if she wasn't the source.

But Brackett was reluctant to leave Maris; he didn't ever want to leave her side again. Daybreak saw this too, and said, "Go on. You have to. One more time. I promise no harm will come to her."

He stood up. "Thanks, Daybreak." It came from the bottom of his heart.

She simply smiled.

"I'll send Doc Milby," he vowed on his way out.

He stepped back out into the windblown winter rain, pausing to retrieve the Porterhouse, wiping it off on the sleeve of his coat, and checking the firing pin before snugging it back under his arm. Stepping to Irish, he felt again for a pulse, found it, and thanked God again.

"I thought you Irishmen were supposed to be tough *hombres*," he said, going down on his knees in the mire to roll Kempen over. "And here you are. You take one bullet and you act like you're going to die on me." He got his arms under Kempen, locked his back and lifted with his legs. "This is the thanks I get for hiring you?" He carried the wounded man to the porch, staggering under the load, and then almost slipped laying Kempen down. Sitting there a moment to catch his breath, Brackett looked down at his friend and felt a burning behind his eyes. "What the hell is wrong with you?" His voice was ragged. "Why don't you say something, dammit? You were always quick to talk back to me before."

"Be quiet," croaked Irish, too tired to open his eyes.

Grinning like a cat, Brackett got up and strode with new vigor to the back of the dogtrot. As Reese had said, there were two horses over by the woodpile, the reins weighed down with pieces of firewood. He took the one wearing Reese's fancy saddle. Riding around the house and turning onto the road, he spotted Doc Milby slogging through the mud, grip in hand. Brackett smiled. The old sawbones always rode to the sound of guns. Only this time he hadn't paused to have his buggy hitched up. Milby was puffing like a locomotive on an upgrade—it was a handsome run all the way here from his office in the middle of town. But Milby was a game old rooster. Seeing Brackett, he stopped to let the marshal ride up alongside. Bent over with his hands on his knees, Milby heaved in air and shot an aggravated look up at Clem.

"My place, Doc."

"I figured as much."

"Maris is hurt. And Irish has been gutshot."

Milby straightened with a groan. "Well, go on. I'll see what I can do for them. Don't want to keep you from your business.

Go make some more work for me."

Brackett kicked the horse forward. As he rode into Two Rivers the angry sky opened up and the rain fell harder, frozen into pelting sleet. Then he heard a flurry of gunshots and saw black smoke, wind-whipped, rise over the rooftops from somewhere down on the Texas Side.

Chapter Twenty-Four

The Texans spent the hour's truce in The Palace.

Hobart was standing out front when they came in grim silence down Smoke Street from their abortive assault on the jail. Seeing Banks draped over the saddle, the saloon owner said, "Bring him in out of the weather. Drinks on the house, gents," and then went inside. The cowboys exchanged a few curious looks. Davis nodded the okay and a pair of drovers carried Lon into the saloon. The rest tied up their horses, grabbed their rifles, and followed.

Hobart walked back behind the bar and began to line up bottles of whiskey from one end to the other. Some of the trail hands unstacked the furniture and sat down. Others preferred to remain at the bar. A couple muttered "Thanks" to Hobart as they snatched up a bottle. A few more labored to build smokes from damp makings. Rain poured off their slickers to puddle on the floor. Banks was stretched out on the mahogany. Kane came in last and caught the arm of one of the Triangle boys as the latter escorted a bottle across the room.

"Take it outside, Jube. Keep an eye on things."

Jube went out reluctantly and Kane stepped to the bar across from Hobart. He looked down the line of men and then at the saloonkeeper.

"What are you doing?" he queried, suspicious.

"They'd take it anyway," shrugged Hobart, putting a full bottle of Valley Tan in front of Kane. "I might as well give it to them."

Jube, slanted up against the front of the saloon, was half finished with his own bottle and was starting to feel right with the world and ambivalent about the storm when he saw a man in black coming down the boardwalk on this side of the street. Sobering quickly, the cowboy pushed away and peered through the gloom a moment, then hurried inside.

"Somebody's coming," he announced.

Everybody looked around at him—everybody except Davis and Kane. Davis was watching Kane, and Kane appeared to be studying the label on his bottle.

"Who is it?" asked Davis.

"Can't say for certain. Man in a black coat, carrying a rifle. I think it's that lawman."

"We'll have to kill him," Davis muttered.

"We've come too far now to do anything but," said Kane flatly. He shoved away from the bar and stalked outside, brushing Jube aside.

Stanhouse watched the men file out and crowd The Palace boardwalk. His step did not falter. As he passed in front of the Lone Star Dancehall, Sulky appeared in the doorway.

"What's going on?" asked the bouncer.

"Time to dust out," advised Stanhouse amiably. "Any girls left in there, you'd be wise to send them packing."

"They're all gone," lamented Sulky.

"They've got better sense."

Sulky resented that. "I'm paid to watch out for this place."

"There's nothing left to watch over, man."

Sulky looked down the street at the tight bunch of trail hands a few boardwalks south.

"What are you doing?"

"Cashing in," said Stanhouse wryly, and walked on.

When the gambler reached the boardwalk of the building adjacent to The Palace, Tyler Kane, in front of the others, snapped, "That's far enough," and Stanhouse stopped. He held the Winchester 44/40 loosely in his right hand.

"You're not the marshal," murmured Kane.

"Not hardly."

"That's the cardsharp that killed your man," vouched one of the RD Connected boys. "I was here last night. I'm a witness."

"Stanhouse," breathed Kane.

"And you're Tyler Kane. I find it amusing that you didn't know me, sir. After all the trouble you've gone to. You've wanted me dead for two years, and all that time you didn't even know what I looked like." Stanhouse shook his head. "Isn't life a funny business?"

"You killed my son," choked Kane.

"I did. I cheated him at cards and then I shot him dead when he took offense. So here I am, Mr. Kane. What are you waiting for? You've come a long way for this. I'd wager it has cost you more than you ever imagined it would." Stanhouse prodded with an insolent tone. "What's wrong? This is a fair game. Don't worry about tomorrow. Don't think about what you'll be left with when the deal is over."

Kane stared at Stanhouse like a man entranced.

"What have I done?" he breathed.

Stanhouse brought the repeater to bear, a quick and savage action that provoked a reflex of violent reaction. The gambler got off one shot. The bullet lodged in Tyler Kane's heart and threw him backward. A dozen Texas guns spoke almost as one.

Clyde Hobart barged through the press of crouching cowboys and pulled up short beside the fallen Kane. As the gray and acrid gunsmoke cleared he looked across at the bullet-torn body of Lee Stanhouse sprawled across the next boardwalk. Then he bent down to gently close Kane's sightless eyes.

"He didn't have to cheat to win, after all," he said dully.

Davis pushed forward and viciously brought his knee up to knock Hobart back.

"Get your hands off him," snarled Davis belligerently.

Hobart got to his feet, brushed off his clothes and rearranged his dignity. With stiff and disdainful arrogance he walked through the cowboys and entered The Palace. Without once looking back, he went the length of the saloon to the office. Putting on hat, gloves, and overcoat, he took the strongbox from the bottom desk drawer, opened the window, and slipped out into the storm-lashed obscurity.

"It isn't finished!" Davis raged at the sullen and confused Texans. "This doesn't set things to right."

He scanned their hard-set faces and knew that if he expected these men to follow him he would have to provide more than talk.

"Two of you follow me," he barked, and pushed through them to enter The Palace. A pair of RD Connected men tagged along. Davis pointed at Lon Banks still lying unconscious on the bar. "Get him out of here." The men obeyed, and as they got Banks upright between them Lon began to come out of it. He did a halfway job of walking to the door on his own. Davis moved to the nearest wall-mounted lamp, lifting it from its wrought-iron brace and hurling it at the nearest pile of wrecked furniture. The lamp shattered in a spray of kerosene. Davis struck a match to life on the butt of his sidegun, flicked it, and stepped back as the kerosene ignited into hungry flame. He went back outside.

"I say we burn this town, boys. Let's give 'em something to remember. From now on every trail town from Ogallala to Sedalia will think twice before they muddy our water. They won't soon forget what Two Rivers got for messing with us!"

"Let's get it done," someone muttered.

As one they surged resolutely to their horses, swinging up into wet saddles. Somebody cut loose with a fierce coyote yell and they were off in small groups in all directions. As Davis mounted up, one of his men reined his prancing cowpony alongside. Davis recognized him as one of the pair he had bailed out of jail the day before.

"Luke and I will start with the jail," the man said.

Davis smiled. "Let's ride."

They headed up Smoke at a gallop. Lon Banks remained on the boardwalk of The Palace for a dazed moment. Behind him, inside, the fire was spreading rapidly, a roaring inferno. He could feel its hellish heat as he stared groggily at Tyler Kane's body. Without really knowing why, he bent down and got Kane under the arms and dragged him off the boardwalk. The effort made his head swim, and he sat down hard in the mud and dry-heaved. Belatedly he realized that two riders had checked their horses behind him. He twisted around and looked up, blinking into the sleet.

It was Carson and Yuby.

Lon stared dumbly at them.

Magruder cleared the door of the jail and rolled out onto the boardwalk as Davis and his two men brought their horses to a halt. The brace of Dance revolvers lay in his lap.

"Get that one-eyed bastard out here now!" demanded Davis.

"He's long gone."

"I'll see for myself," sneered Davis, and was making to dismount when Magruder brought the revolvers up to bear. Immediately the RD Connected men put stocks to shoulders and aimed their rifles at Magruder. In that instant Magruder heard a shoe scuff against wood, and crooked his body to look back at Davey Lake in the doorway.

"I told you to get out the back way, boy!" he bellowed. "Now do as I say and run!"

But Davey stood there, staring at the rifles.

"Get the hell out of here!" snarled Davis.

"I ain't afraid of you!" cried Davey defiantly.

Magruder threw his guns away to either side. "No shooting," he sighed.

Davis finished his dismount. His men lowered their rifles. Davis considered Magruder a moment with a frosty smile, then said, with cold malice, "Move him out of the way."

One of the cowboys untied his lass-rope. With one stern jerk of his arm, he shook the loop out and made his throw. Magruder stiffened as the loop snaked down over him, and he shot a look of contempt at Davis.

"'The expense of spirit in a waste of shame,'" he said.

The cowboy yanked the rope taut, made a quick dally around his saddlehorn and dug spur. Magruder gasped as the rope constricted about his chest; he gripped the wheels as though he thought he might hold the chair fast in that way. And then, with a savage wrench he was hauled forward, lashed to the wheelchair. The ground came up to meet him, and the cold mud blinded him and filled his mouth, bouncing his head back brutally. The top of the chair was driven downward and cleanly snapped his spine.

Davey Lake lunged forward with an incoherent cry, reaching out as though to grab hold of the wheelchair, but he wasn't fast enough, and Davis stepped in and caught him. A shot rang out. Davis pivoted to see the cowboy who was giving Magruder the lethal "Texas sleigh ride" launched sideways out of his saddle. The horse kept going, straight down Smoke, wheelchair and dead man sledding along behind, laying a deep furrow in the street. Davis looked left and saw Brackett charging up Main at a hard gallop, Remington in hand. An instinct for preservation caused him to swing Davey roughly in front of him. Brackett saw this even as he checked his horse sharply and dismounted on the run. The horse lost its footing in the half-frozen mire, fell on its side, thrashed violently and rose up into the second cowboy's line of fire. Davis had a better angle, and fired his sidegun. Brackett swung that way, crouching in the middle of the street, and cursed, for the struggling boy was still in the way. The horse, snorting, gave a kick and trotted resentfully back down Main. Now the RD Connected hand had a clear shot. His rifle kicked and barked. The bullet tugged at Brackett's coat as the lawman moved, fanning the hammer of the Remington. The drover did a backward flip off his horse, the rifle hurled from a dead hand.

Davis fired again. The impact spun Brackett around as a hot

212

numbness swept through his left arm. Davey thrashed hysterically and twisted half out of Davis's grasp, and Riley surrendered his hold in order to steady his aim, tossing the boy roughly off the boardwalk. Davey sprawled facedown in the muddy street. Brackett spun and fired twice more, but Davis had moved. One bullet splintered an upright, the other smacked into the brick of the wall. Brackett triggered again; the hammer fell on an empty chamber.

"That's six!" cried Davis in a wild exultation as he straightened to aim his next shot more carefully.

Brackett dropped the Remington, pulled the Porterhouse .37 from under his coat and fired.

Riley Davis pitched forward, catching the tie rail with his shoulder and jacknifing into the slime.

Two-thirds of the way down Smoke, Yuby saw the riderless horse galloping toward him, dragging the wheelchair with a man bound to it. Alive or dead, Wellman couldn't tell, but the cruel indignity of it brought the bitter taste of bile to his mouth. He drew his sidegun, aimed, and fired two shots. The horse died instantly, nosediving into the mud. The rope slackened and the wheelchair bounced twice before landing upright. Magruder's head lolled forward to lay in a grotesquely unnatural way on his unmoving chest.

At the same moment a pair of RD Connected drovers spurred their horses single-file up across the boardwalk of the Lone Star Dancehall and through the double doors. Glass shattered, and one door, splintering, parted company with its hinges and spun like a top before crashing to the floor. A heartbeat later Sulky was there, rushing forward with joy lighting up his face and his fists ready to strike. But the bouncer had never before been confronted by an adversary on horseback. It occurred to him that there was one simple way to remove this obstacle. He put everything he had into the haymaker that caught the nearest horse solidly just forward of the throatlatch. The animal staggered and went down, its rider kicking clear and scudding across the floor on his rump.

Astonished, the other horseman gaped at Sulky and said, "That's just the damndest thing I ever saw."

But the cowboy on the floor was not amused. He rolled over and saw the biggest brute he had ever laid eyes on coming at him. He fumbled for his gun and pointed it at Sulky and cried, "Stand back!", but Sulky flashed a happy grin and reached down to lift the drover as easily as if he were a bag of feathers. The RD Connected man fired twice at point-blank range. Sulky roared like an enraged bull grizzly and hurled the trail hand through the plate glass window thirty feet away and then turned to advance on the second cowboy, but the felled horse was getting back up, clumsy and graceless on the worn-slick dancehall floor, and Sulky collided blindly with it, spun away, and died before falling.

The second man dismounted, hazed the two horses out the doorway, and cautiously drew his sidegun before going over to prod Sulky with the toe of his boot. The bouncer was well past the point of taking issue, so the drover stepped back out onto the boardwalk to see his saddle partner strewn unconscious across the planking. He took a step that way before catching movement out of an eye corner, and whirled to face Brackett, who stood out in the street beyond a silver-gray curtain of sleet.

"Drop the gun," demanded Brackett.

The cowboy glanced down at the thumb-buster in his grasp; he had half-forgotten drawing it.

Brackett started toward him, the mud sucking at his bootheels, a throbbing, teeth-gritting pain spreading through his shoulder, radiating from the slug of lead buried deep in his torn flesh. For one brief, searing instant of madness and disgust he was possessed by a poisonous contempt for this man and his foolish, dangerous, destructive pride. He wanted to break that high-mettled cowboy vanity into pieces, for it was pride that had invited so much death and ruin to Two Rivers.

So he advanced, prodding this man, pushing into his space and applying relentless pressure on his pride. The man turned pale and stepped back until he fetched up against the wall of the Lone Star and could retreat no further.

"Put it down," snarled Brackett, "or I'll kill you."

He raised the Porterhouse.

"No!" The cowboy, unnerved into irrational panic, fired and fell sideways simultaneously. Brackett fired a half-second later, but he did not move or flinch. This was his winning edge, acquired from a lifetime of facing prideful men with guns. He wasn't one to shoot and dodge at the same time. The cowboy's shot went wild. Brackett's aim was true, slamming the drover down. Dying spasms set his bootheels drumming on the boards. And then death released him.

Jube checked his running horse to a slippery stop in front of the Lone Star. He had witnessed the shootout. Brackett slowly turned his head to look blankly at the Triangle rider. The loosely held Porterhouse dangled at his side, and he made no move to lift it.

"That was murder!" cried Jube. "I seen it. You push too damned hard, lawman!"

Brackett said nothing. He could scarcely deny it.

Jube raised his rifle.

Down the street, Wellman fired again.

Jube leaned forward, then slipped slowly from the saddle to splash into the street.

"Christ," muttered Brackett, sick of killing to the depths of his soul.

Lon Banks got to his feet, swaying like a drunken man. "Yuby," he slurred disbelieving, "you backshooting sonuva . . ."

The charred remains of The Palace's roof caved in with a rending crash that shook the earth and sent bolts of fire out into the street and a swarm of burning embers skyward. Already the building just south of the saloon was ablaze. Lon was hammered forward onto his knees by the fiery blast. Yuby's horse bucked and pivoted, frightened by the noise and the heat. Lon pulled his gun. Yuby got off one shot, but the bronco antics of the claybank spoiled his aim.

"Banks!"

Lon's head swiveled. At first he saw only a riderless horse, then the horse whirled away and Carson was standing there in the street, the Henry repeater at hip level. Banks swung the gun around.

The Henry spoke, jumping in Carson's steady hands.

Up at the Lone Star, Brackett steadied himself against an upright and scanned the sleet-pounded street. Several horses loped aimlessly through the mire, saddles empty. He spotted a couple of riders drifting away like ghosts into the wet gloom of the alleys, and several more at the end of Smoke, disappearing onto Kiowa. Cattle bawled way down at the stockyards. The fire started at The Palace crackled and roared and leap-frogged, wind-driven southward from structure to tinderbox structure. The Texas Side was going up in smoke, but the norther would blow the fire away from the deadline.

Brackett turned and headed home.

Epilogue

The fire on the Texas Side raged for hours and consumed all of the buildings on the east side of Smoke from The Palace to Kiowa Street. The norther threw drifts of embers across Kiowa and the tracks of the Chicago & North Western railroad, along with dense and acrid clouds of smoke, and these combined to incite the Texas longhorns in the stockyards to panic. Hundreds of head were trampled to death in the breakout and stampede that ensued. Many were convinced that it had to be the biggest stampede in the history of the West. Thousands scattered across the plains, and carried with them the herds held south of the Platte River. Some were recovered, but not nearly all. The big losers were the cattle buyers and their clients, who had already taken delivery and paid off. The big winners were the sodbusters in the vicinity; a great many homesteading families dined well on beefsteak that winter.

Carson Kane and Yuby Wellman had a bad moment when, returning to the Triangle camp, they found the Studebaker chuckwagon demolished into so much kindling, having been caught in the path of the stampeding herd. But Banjo Stubbins proved to be a man who could recognize trouble when it came thundering down on him. Snatching up thirty-three feet of Brazos lariat, the resourceful waddy had thrown a line over the lower limb of a cottonwood and shinnied to the safety of this high perch with remarkable agility for someone carrying so many hard years.

Seeing Tyler Kane buried in Two Rivers' boot hill right alongside Murdoch's grave in a plot of Nebraska dirt that Kane had once measured for Lee Stanhouse, Carson rode home to Texas, accompanied by Yuby and Banjo and a handful of sheepish Triangle cowboys. He introduced shorthorn cattle to his spread and made a decent living. Around the turn of the century, in the autumn of his life, Carson Kane became a very wealthy and powerful individual, for oil was struck on the Triangle, and in abundance.

For all intents and purposes, Two Rivers ceased to be a cattle town. Eventually the railroad extended westward. In time folks got out of the habit of calling the district south of Main Street by names like Little Texas and the Texas Side. But Smoke Street and Yellowtooth Road never did become entirely respectable. Farmers, rather than cowboys, became accustomed to seeking their pleasures and pampering their vices in the sourmash mills and cathouses of the south side. The farmers proved to be less inclined to noise and violence—that was the substantial difference.

Clyde Hobart was never seen in Two Rivers again. He was next heard of operating a saloon in San Francisco that was popular with the mining crews, and he spent much of his leisure time on the east side of Dupont, in Chinatown.

Daybreak Magruder maintained the boarding house on Yellowtooth. The rumor persisted, as the most vicious rumors do, that the Magruder house was in reality a brothel. But in fact it served only to room the girls of easy virtue and poor prospects who plied their trade in other south side establishments, a subtle distinction that the reputable citizenry as a whole willfully disregarded.

Irish Joe Kempen recovered fully from his gunshot wound. He became the marshal at Two Rivers, and occasionally, when in the night his instincts would lead him to Yellowtooth, he would drop in at the Magruder house and relax for an hour or two of friendly conversation with Daybreak in the book-lined study on the first floor.

Clem Brackett gave his badge and his notice to Leon McKaskle the day after the Texas Side fire. He purchased a parcel of land some twenty miles from Two Rivers, to which he and Maris moved shortly after the birth of their first son, Joseph Magruder Brackett. Acquiring an army contract to provide cavalry remounts, Brackett settled into a fairly peaceful and productive existence. Only once, some years later—and with reluctance—was he compelled to pick up his guns and leave, for a time, his wife's side.

Patch Russell reappeared, briefly, at Eli's Livery, the day of the shootout on Smoke Street. Kesserling, bound and gagged and locked in the tack room, was able to peek through a knothole in the wall and so was later able to relate that Russell slipped furtively into the livery that cold, wet, and gloomy afternoon. The horse that the gunslinger Reese had bought from Eli—the one that Brackett had ridden into battle with the Texans—had, as horses are wont to do, returned to the trough, and Eli had stabled it and laid the fancy saddle across the stall gate earlier in the day. It was this saddle instead of his own that Patch Russell put on the back of his spotted gray. It was obvious to Eli that Russell intended to leave Two Rivers with property that wasn't his. But Patch never got the chance.

A man stepped out of the shadows as soon as Russell had cinched that saddle to his horse. According to Eli, this man—the same man who had trussed him up like a turkey come Thanksgiving—looked like a cattleman and talked with a soft Texas drawl. That saddle was his, the man coldly informed Russell. He had been bushwhacked and left for dead, his horse killed under him and his saddle stolen, down near Phantom Hill, Texas. This by a bastard whose trail eventually joined that of a herd being pushed north. The stranger recovered from his injuries and went to tracking, but caught up with the herd only after it had reached Two Rivers. He found his hand-tooled, custom-made, three hundred dollar saddle in Eli's Livery. All he had to do was wait for the lowdown stinking yellow coward who had ambushed him to come and claim it. Patch went to blathering something but couldn't form the words coherently with his ruined mouth. The stranger drew his gun and shot him dead, put that fancy saddle on a big roan gelding, which Eli swore carried a brand he had never seen before, and rode away. He left the old hull he had come in on to Kesserling.

As it turned out, nobody made much of an issue about the slaying of Patch Russell. The snow began to fall that very afternoon, a heavy, silent white blanket that drifted down from a leaden sky for days on end. As the charred ruins along Smoke Street cooled, the snow covered this black and ugly devastation. It covered the Texas-bound tracks of Russell's nameless killer as well, but few argued for pursuit. They called it simple frontier justice.

WESTERN STORYTELLER
ROBERT KAMMEN
ALWAYS DEALS ACES WITH HIS TALES
OF AMERICA'S ROUGH-AND-READY FRONTIER!

DEATH RIDES THE ROCKIES	(2509, $2.95)
DEVIL'S FORD	(2102, $2.50)
GUNSMOKE AT HANGING WOMAN CREEK	(2658, $2.95)
LONG HENRY	(2155, $2.50)
MONTANA SHOWDOWN	(2333, $2.95)
WIND RIVER KILL	(2213, $2.50)
WINTER OF THE BLUE SNOW	(2432, $3.50)
WYOMING GUNSMOKE	(2284, $2.50)

Available wherever paperbacks are sold, or order direct from the Publisher. Send cover price plus 50¢ per copy for mailing and handling to Zebra Books, Dept. 2898, 475 Park Avenue South, New York, N.Y. 10016. Residents of New York, New Jersey and Pennsylvania must include sales tax. DO NOT SEND CASH.

ACTION ADVENTURE: WINGMAN #1–#6
by Mack Maloney

WINGMAN (2015, $3.95)
From the radioactive ruins of a nuclear-devastated U.S. emerges a hero for the ages. A brilliant ace fighter pilot, he takes to the skies to help free his once-great homeland from the brutal heel of the evil Soviet warlords. He is the last hope of a ravaged land. He is Hawk Hunter . . . Wingman!

WINGMAN #2: THE CIRCLE WAR (2120, $3.95)
A second explosive showdown with the Russian overlords and their armies of destruction is in the wind. Only the deadly aerial ace Hawk Hunter can rally the forces of freedom and strike one last blow for a forgotten dream called "America"!

WINGMAN #3: THE LUCIFER CRUSADE (2232, $3.95)
Viktor, the depraved international terrorist who orchestrated the bloody war for America's West, has escaped. Ace pilot Hawk Hunter takes off for a deadly confrontation in the skies above the Middle East.

WINGMAN #4: THUNDER IN THE EAST (2453, $3.95)
The evil New Order is raising a huge mercenary force to reclaim America, and Hawk Hunter, the battered nation's most fearless top gun fighter pilot, takes to the air to prevent this catastrophe from occurring.

WINGMAN #5: THE TWISTED CROSS (2553, $3.95)
"The Twisted Cross," a power-hungry neo-Nazi organization, plans to destroy the Panama Canal with nuclear time bombs unless their war chests are filled with stolen Inca gold. The only route to saving the strategic waterway is from above—as Wingman takes to the air to rain death down upon the Cross' South American jungle stronghold.

WINGMAN #6: THE FINAL STORM (2655, $3.95)
Deep in the frozen Siberian wastes, last-ditch elements of the Evil Empire plan to annihilate the Free World in one final rain of nuclear death. Trading his sleek F-16 fighter jet for a larger, heavier B-1B supersonic swing-wing bomber, Hawk Hunter undertakes his most perilous mission.

Available wherever paperbacks are sold, or order direct from the Publisher. Send cover price plus 50¢ per copy for mailing and handling to Zebra Books, Dept. 2898, 475 Park Avenue South, New York, N.Y. 10016. Residents of New York, New Jersey and Pennsylvania must include sales tax. DO NOT SEND CASH.

MYSTERIES TO KEEP YOU GUESSING
by John Dickson Carr

CASTLE SKULL (1974, $3.50)
The hand may be quicker than the eye, but ghost stories didn't hoodwink Henri Bencolin. A very real murderer was afoot in Castle Skull—a murderer who must be found before he strikes again.

IT WALKS BY NIGHT (1931, $3.50)
The police burst in and found the Duc's severed head staring at them from the center of the room. Both the doors had been guarded, yet the murderer had gone in and out *without having been seen*!

THE EIGHT OF SWORDS (1881, $3.50)
The evidence showed that while waiting to kill Mr. Depping, the murderer had calmly eaten his victim's dinner. But before famed crime-solver Dr. Gideon Fell could serve up the killer to Scotland Yard, there would be another course of murder.

THE MAN WHO COULD NOT SHUDDER (1703, $3.50)
Three guests at Martin Clarke's weekend party swore they saw the pistol lifted from the wall, levelled, and shot. *Yet no hand held it*. It couldn't have happened—but there was a dead body on the floor to prove that it had.

Available wherever paperbacks are sold, or order direct from the Publisher. Send cover price plus 50¢ per copy for mailing and handling to Zebra Books, Dept. 2898, 475 Park Avenue South, New York, N.Y. 10016. Residents of New York, New Jersey and Pennsylvania must include sales tax. DO NOT SEND CASH.

THE ONLY ALTERNATIVE IS ANNIHILATION...
RICHARD P. HENRICK

SILENT WARRIORS (3026, $4.50)
The Red Star, Russia's newest, most technologically advanced submarine, outclasses anything in the U.S. fleet. But when the captain opens his sealed orders 24 hours early, he's staggered to read that he's to spearhead a massive nuclear first strike against the Americans!

THE PHOENIX ODYSSEY (2858, $4.50)
All communications to the USS *Phoenix* suddenly and mysteriously vanish. Even the urgent message from the president cancelling the War Alert is not received. In six short hours the *Phoenix* will unleash its nuclear arsenal against the Russian mainland.

COUNTERFORCE (3025, $4.50)
In the silent deep, the chase is on to save a world from destruction. A single Russian Sub moves on a silent and sinister course for American shores. The men aboard the U.S.S. *Triton* must search for and destroy the Soviet killer Sub as an unsuspecting world races for the apocalypse.

CRY OF THE DEEP (2594, $3.95)
With the Supreme leader of the Soviet Union dead the Kremlin is pointing a collective accusing finger towards the United States. The motherland wants revenge and unless the U.S. Swordfish can stop the Russian Caspian, the salvoes of World War Three are a mere heartbeat away!

BENEATH THE SILENT SEA (2423, $3.95)
The Red Dragon, Communist China's advanced ballistic missile-carrying submarine embarks on the most sinister mission in human history: to attack the U.S. and Soviet Union simultaneously. Soon, the Russian Barkal, with its planned attack on a single U.S. sub is about unwittingly to aid in the destruction of all of mankind!

Available wherever paperbacks are sold, or order direct from the Publisher. Send cover price plus 50¢ per copy for mailing and handling to Zebra Books, Dept. 2898, 475 Park Avenue South, New York, N.Y. 10016. Residents of New York, New Jersey and Pennsylvania must include sales tax. DO NOT SEND CASH.